ALSO BY C. J. DAUGHERTY

Night School
Night School: Legacy
Night School: Fracture
Night School: Resistance
Night School: Endgame

The Secret Fire
The Secret City

AS CHRISTI DAUGHERTY

The Echo Killing
A Beautiful Corpse
Revolver Road

NIGHT SCHOOL: THE SHORT STORIES
By C. J. Daugherty

Copyright © 2020 Moonflower Books Ltd.
www.cjdaugherty.com

ISBN: 9781838237400

Published by Moonflower Books Ltd

Designed and set by Jasmine Aurora
www.jasmineaurora.co.uk

Cover image and illustrations by Shutterstock

NIGHT SCHOOL
The SHORT STORIES

C. J. DAUGHERTY

MOONFLOWER

Contents

Introduction

Ever since I first began writing *Night School*, I've written 'extra' pieces, mostly for myself. Basically, I have a habit of writing too much and then cutting back until only the heart of the story is left. The extra pieces I keep, like a seamstress hordes scraps of fabric in case one day she can use them to make a quilt. In that case, you might say this book is my quilt.

This book contains my favourite short stories, reverse perspective chapters, and out-takes. None of them made the final books, and yet I love them all the same. Some of these I've put on my website for readers to discover. Others I've tucked away and all but forgotten about. A few have never before seen the light of day. One of these is the original paranormal draft of *Night School*. I kept it just in case I ever wanted to write about vampires and witches. I still might write that book someday. In the meantime, I wanted you to see how it all began. Similarly, *Strange as Angels* could have been book 2 in that unfinished series had it all worked out, and I've included an excerpt from that for you to read.

You'll notice some of the characters in those early drafts have the same names I ultimately used in Night School, but they sound and act quite differently here. So don't be surprised. First looks and last glances are often very different things. It's kind of fun to see how things started, and compare it to how they ended up.

These old versions may still be pillaged for a future series, but they will never be published exactly as they are here, so this is your only chance to see what might have been. And how Night School evolved from those early versions.

It was a real joy to put this together, creating a book out of the odds and ends I had stored in drawers and file folders. It is always a pleasure to spend a few hours back at Cimmeria Academy. I hope you like it, too.

Always,
C.J.

The Prequel

I've been asked many times to write about Allie Sheridan's life before Night School. This prequel is one of very few occasions when I've actually done it. That said, I've always had a very clear picture of her back then. To me she was the classic good girl gone bad — a decent student and pleasant daughter and sister who lost her way after life dealt her a blow too vicious for her to process, and then the adults in her life let her down.

This short story came to me one afternoon when I was supposed to be writing something else entirely. Suddenly, I had this image of Allie at fifteen — bitter and furious, looking for something to kick. I found myself writing it very quickly, even though I had no place to use it. Once it was finished, I just put it away. It was good to know about past Allie for myself, but I didn't think anyone else would be interested. Since then, the story has sat around, hidden in the depths of my hard drive, until now.

It tells the story of Allie's first day at Brixton Hill School. And goes, I think, some way toward explaining why her parents are so weary and frustrated at the start of Night School.

There's no question, Allie breaking bad is a force of nature. But then, as you and I know, she has her reasons.

So here's Allie, losing her way. And making the kind of friends it would be nice to go to jail with.

I hope you like it.

Lowering her heavily painted eyelids, Allie turned to face the dark haired boy. "Haven't you ever seen a girl before? Jesus."

I'm In

– ALLIE –

"I see your record at your last school was … problematic." As he spoke, the headmaster peered at Allie over the tops of his glasses.

Perched on a dingy plastic seat facing his desk – with its ostentatious sign reading "Headmaster Ross" in block letters – Allie affected boredom as she studied her sparkly purple nails.

They need to be filed, she noticed absently. *Must do that.*

He was still talking. "I've seen your previous records, though, and I know you are capable of better things. You were a high achiever just over a year ago – on your way to university and then who knows what kind of brilliant career. But it's as if your marks went off a cliff."

That's actually a pretty good way of putting it, Ross-o. Her eyes skittered off his face.

She thought he was strangely unattractive, with bulging eyes and a bald head that was perfectly egg-shaped. But he didn't seem unkind.

"That doesn't just occur in a vacuum," he said. "What happened, Alyson?"

She looked back down at her nails.

After an uncomfortable pause, he continued. "Your parents have sent you here because they're hoping teachers who are skilled in working with difficult children will be able to help you."

"I'm not a child."

It was the first thing Allie had said since she'd walked into his office and for a moment he blinked at her in surprise.

"You're fifteen years old, Alyson."

"So what?" She raised her resentful grey eyes to meet his gaze. "That's a number. It doesn't make me a child."

"Then what are you?" He leaned back in his battered black faux-leather chair, crossing his hands across his narrow waist. "Because you're certainly not an adult."

"I am," she said after deliberation, "an angry young woman."

"Our teachers can work with those, too," he said dryly. "Follow me and I'll introduce you to them."

Sighing dramatically, Allie stood, flipping her arrow-straight, jet-black hair out of her eyes. She'd dyed it yesterday in honour of her first day at her new school. Her mother had been furious.

At least she noticed.

Someone had painted the walls of Brixton Hill School a pale olive green; it gave the hallway a vaguely militaristic look. The painting had clearly happened some time ago, though, as the walls were scuffed and dusty. Spots of brighter paint showed where something – graffiti probably – had been more recently covered up.

The linoleum floor was stained and dirty, and dead bugs slowly decayed overhead in the covers of the fluorescent strip lights. It all conspired to give the building a depressing, muddy hue. It felt like the last school at the end of the world.

This place is awesome. Thanks, Mum and Dad. I'm sure I'll get the best education here and go on to do great things with my life...

Allie's resentful thoughts stopped as the headmaster tapped on a white door with a square window. The paint was flaking off it in chunks.

The door opened just a little, and a small woman looked up at him through the crack. She was unnaturally thin, her wiry black hair shot through with threads of grey. Her skin seemed to sag on her face, as if it had given up. As she peered at him, her expression was weary.

"Headmaster Ross," she said. Her eyes skipped to Allie's face and then back again to his. "The new student?"

"Mrs Williams," he said, "this is Alyson Sheridan. Alyson, Mrs Williams will be teaching you English and History."

With a look on her face that said admitting another truculent teenager into her classroom was the last thing she needed right now, Mrs Williams held the door wider for Allie to pass through.

Inside, the room was crowded with students in a varying array of rebellious attire. Allie was surprised to see so many in one room – the class was even bigger than those at her last school. It smelled of sweat and cheap perfume.

"There's a seat at the back," Mrs Williams said. "I suggest you take it. And watch your bag. They steal."

With that endorsement ringing in her ears, Allie stepped over the legs stuck out into the aisle, and around the backpacks that spilled their contents onto the floor to a wobbly desk in the middle of the room.

Two boys sat next to it. One had a narrow, interesting face, with sharp eyes and shaggy hair dyed jet black, much like Allie's. The other had chubby cheeks and spots. He'd bleached his hair pure white and added a blue streak to one side.

Both of them openly stared at Allie, as she sat down without acknowledging them and pulled out her notebook.

Her skin crawled with the sensation of being observed.

"What are you staring at?" Lowering her heavily painted eyelids, Allie turned to face the dark haired boy. "Haven't you ever seen a girl before? Jesus."

Undaunted, he continued to stare.

"What did you do?" Blue Streak asked her.

With exaggerated patience, she turned to face him. He had a perpetual mischievous expression. Something was tattooed on his hands but Allie couldn't quite make it out.

"I don't understand the question." Her voice was flat.

"He means to get in here." Black Hair was studying her, his gaze steady but curious. "You have to do something to get in here."

"I set my mum on fire." Allie said coldly. "And fed her to the nanny."

Blue Streak smiled at Black Hair. "I don't think she likes us."

Black Hair gave an impatient shrug. "She doesn't know us yet." He turned back to Allie. "It's just a question."

Allie sighed. "Nothing."

"What kind of nothing?" Black Hair pressed her.

Under cover of her mascara-caked lashes, she studied him. She could see the small holes in the worn material of his black T-shirt, which bore the message "Kill Your Heroes" in faded white letters. A skinny white knee poked through a rip in his jeans. The dyed hair cast his pale skin in stark relief; his complexion was like china. She noticed that his fingers twitched with repressed anxiety. His nails had been chewed to the quick.

"The kind of nothing in which you don't go to school when you're meant to," Allie said. She added, unnecessarily, "I have a bad attitude."

He nodded as if he'd suspected as much.

"What about you?" Her voice held a challenge.

"I graffiti things." He sounded proud. "I'm quite well known, actually. He..." – he pointed at Blue Streak – "has an anger problem."

Blue Streak grinned at her broadly. He was missing a tooth on the right side.

Black Hair was still looking at her. "What's your name?"

As usual, she thought about lying. Sometimes she did, but it could get confusing and today she didn't really care what people called her.

"Allie."

"I'm Mark." He pointed at the boy with the blue streak. "This one's Harry."

Allie nodded, but before she could speak, Mrs Williams called for quiet in a shrill voice, and she turned to face her.

Mark touched her arm to get her attention – his fingertips were calloused but his touch was surprisingly gentle. She glanced at him.

"You should come out with us tonight," he whispered.

"Where?" she whispered back, frowning.

His smile was impishly crooked. "Does it matter?"

Mrs Williams was still talking but Allie wasn't hearing a word she said. Nothing teachers had to say interested her these days.

When she glanced back up at Mark, he was still watching her expectantly. There was something in his eyes. A kind of … hope, maybe. An offer of friendship. A connection.

After a long pause, she inclined her head very slightly.

"OK," she said. "I'm in."

Carter's View at the Pond

I don't think it's wrong to say that the skinny-dipping scene in Night School book 1 has become a bit iconic among true fans. It's the first time we see Carter as both a practical and a romantic hero. Allie, understandably freaked out about being naked in a pond with everyone in her class (just thinking about doing that makes me have a panic attack) has an actual panic attack, and can't breathe. Lost in the crowd she almost drowns until Carter notices her going under, and talks her into breathing again.

I love this scene. Not just because it brings these characters together in a way that feels fateful, but also because it's based on things that *really happen*.

As some of you know, I live in the south of England, surrounded by boarding schools. These schools that look like palaces fascinate me. I went to high school in Texas, in a school that looked like a juvenile detention centre across the street from a muffler shop and a Wendy's hamburger place. Don't get me wrong, it was a good school and I loved it. But it didn't look anything like a castle. And I met people who went to school in these castles and one of the stories they told me was that in the summer (school in England runs through July) they would have mass skinny-dipping swims as a class on certain dates. This was a school tradition at several boarding schools. That stayed with me because the most bonding we did in my high school was at the Friday morning pep rally.

When I was writing Night School, I always knew I'd add a skinny-dipping scene. And if you think it couldn't happen in real life... Think again.

Here's a reverse perspective of the Summer Splash, from Carter's point of view.

Reaching down into the

dark water, he caught

her upper arms,

yanking her roughly

from the depths.

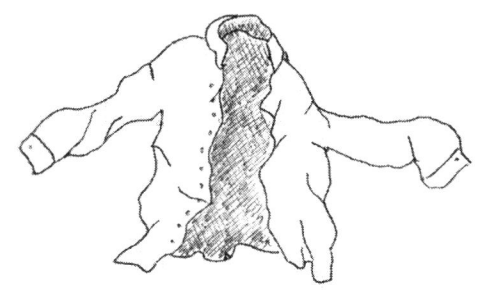

Just Breathe
- CARTER -

Almost invisible in the night, Carter crouched low behind a soft, protective veil of tall ferns. His eyes, familiar with the darkness, swept the landscape with professional suspicion.

He couldn't see the others easily but he could find them if he needed to. A hedge moved against the breeze. A tree trunk failed to hide an expanse of pale leg.

They weren't really trying to hide. All around him he could hear the hiss of whispers and the repressed giggles as his entire class waited for the signal to drop their clothes and jump into cold water.

He sighed, rocking back on his heels, arms crossed.

The Summer Splash. Was there anything more ridiculous at Cimmeria Academy? Anything more juvenile and idiotic?

Lips tight, he shook his head as if there might be someone near enough to see his disapproval. To know he was not voluntarily a part of this teenage lunacy.

I should be in my room, he thought. *Sleeping or reading. Anything but this.*

And yet, here he was, contemplating joining in. All because he knew she was here.

Somewhere in the darkness, Allie was hiding.

He knew she didn't want to be here any more than he did. He'd seen the expression on her face when Jo had explained the rules of the game. First, she'd looked aghast. And then, when she saw Jo's enthusiasm, resigned.

Peer pressure, he thought, looking with accusing eyes at the hiding places surrounding him. That was the problem. Half the people hiding right now wouldn't be here at all were it not for their friends making them do it.

Who in their right mind, would think this was a good idea? he wondered. *Hey, I'm not insecure enough in my day-to-day school life. I think I'll stand naked in front of the entire school tonight. For kicks.*

He'd always avoided the summer splash. Sneering to himself as the others sneaked out on the same night every year to skinny-dip *en masse*.

But tonight, he'd climbed out of bed and crept down one of the old servants' staircases, making his way through the silent hallways of the school's Gothic mansion, fully aware that dozens of others would be doing the same thing, all to come stand here in the dark.

His stomach felt tight with nerves. He still hadn't yet decided whether he'd join in.

He really didn't want to. *Sod it. What the hell am I even doing here?*

That was the question of the hour.

Was he here to help Allie if something went wrong? Or because he hoped to see her naked? At the thought, heat rose to his face. *Little of both I guess.*

He pounded his fist quietly against the soft earth at his feet.

God, he was such a glutton for punishment. Why was he doing this to himself? She didn't fancy him. She'd made that very clear. And that was just fine with him.

Anyone who'd voluntarily go out with that arrogant, self-obsessed tosser, Sylvain Cassel…

Somewhere in the darkness someone snickered openly.

Carter's gaze snapped towards the sound. Nothing moved. He couldn't be certain where the laugh had originated. Sound carried oddly over water.

When nothing else happened, he relaxed again, letting his thoughts return to the subject that seemed to occupy his mind too much lately.

Why did Allie like Sylvain?

Fine, he was good looking. If you liked cheekbones and blue eyes. But he was also a wanker. Everyone knew it. He was spoiled and rude, and far too aware of his own bone structure. Shouldn't that matter to her? Couldn't she see it?

But he'd seen the look on Allie's face when Sylvain turned on the French charm. When he smiled that hundred-watt smile.

She was dazzled.

Carter couldn't understand her. She was obviously smart. She should be able to see right through Sylvain's tortured soul act.

He sighed.

Jo didn't help, of course. Fluffy, silly Jo. "Let's all have boyfriends together. Ours can both be shallow-with-muscles. Hooray!"

He'd been crouching too long, and his legs were starting to go numb. He shifted position, dropping onto one knee, his movements as silent and sure as a cat's. Now he could rest his elbow on his thigh and prop his chin on his hand as he waited for something to happen. But the night seemed quieter than ever.

His thoughts returned to the problem at hand. The real question was – if he didn't fancy Allie – and he didn't – why did he care who she went out with? Why did it bother him that she chose Sylvain?

He couldn't answer that.

There was something about her. The way she wore too much make-up sometimes and looked like she didn't care what anyone thought. The way she ran with the wind in her hair. The way Katie and her clique picked on her. And the way she always fought back. Fists curled at her sides, ready to swing. To take on anyone.

She was fierce.

And something about that felt … familiar. Like he just knew her. Like they were the same.

The fire inside him was drawn to the fire inside her.

Swallowing hard, he let that thought evaporate.

What is wrong with me tonight?

In the distance, the pond was still. Its surface glittered like black glass. The marsh hens and ducks all slept, unaware their rest was about to be disturbed by a school of teenage lunatics.

Across the water he could just make out the old cottage, so overgrown with vines it barely seemed to have walls. Isabelle always talked about fixing it up but year after year went by and nothing ever happened...

Suddenly, from somewhere very nearby, a deep male voice split the silence. "It's time, kids. Drop trou."

The giggles and whispers rose to a chorus. He could hear the rustling as the students, still in the safety of their hiding places, disrobed.

Despite himself, Carter's heart thumped.

They were really going to do this.

Doubtful, he glanced down at his own shorts and T-shirt. Hiding here and watching everyone else run around naked would be kind of creepy. He had to either join in or leave.

For a long second he hesitated.

"God's sake," he muttered to himself. He pulled his shirt over his head in a single quick movement. His skin seemed unnaturally pale in the darkness, and he glanced down at it with sudden doubt.

Night School training had left his body muscled and lean, but still. He didn't like parading around in front of...

"Now."

The command seemed to come from nowhere and everywhere at once. It was irresistible. Irrefutable. You were either in this thing now or you were out of it.

He heard the first feet pounding on the shore. The first shrieks and then, seconds later, the first splash as bodies hit the water.

Screams of laughter.

His fingers suddenly numb, he fumbled with the buttons on his trousers, dropping them and his underwear in a single movement, and kicking off his shoes.

More screams and splashing.

The night was warm but Carter shivered anyway as he stepped out from behind the waist-high ferns into a bizarre scene of naked bodies hurtling through the dark woods, like one of those old Italian movies.

Before he could decide what to do next, three girls ran by him.

It was Allie, Jo and Lisa.

In the dark madness of the night, they never saw him.

Carter drew in his breath as he watched their flight, their hair streaming behind them. They held hands as they sped towards the water.

Jo was laughing wildly. Lisa's smile was stiff and nervous. But Allie's face held a look of grim determination. Like this was another test she had to pass.

Her skin was like milk.

At the edge of the pond they leapt into the air. Jo giggled shrilly, then disappeared beneath the black water.

For a long moment, Carter couldn't seem to move.

Then someone punched his shoulder roughly, jarring him from his reverie. "Come on, dude. Don't stand there till your dick falls off. Get going."

Carter whirled to find Lucas grinning at him.

"Race you," Lucas said, ducking as Carter swung a fist at him half-heartedly. Feinting left, he ran to the water's edge, jumping in with a hoarse cry.

Carter followed and prepared to jump in after him.

That was when he noticed her.

Alone in the water, flailing and sputtering, Allie looked terrified. Gasping for breath.

She was going under.

Oh, sodding hell, Carter realised with sudden icy clarity. *She doesn't know how to swim.*

Carter's dive was surgical, a clean arc that left barely a ripple in his wake. Breaking the surface, he swam towards her with efficient, strong strokes, reaching her side just as she disappeared again beneath the waves.

Reaching down into the dark water, he caught her upper arms, yanking her roughly from the depths.

Her skin was cold and slippery, and he had to hold on tight in order not to lose his hold.

She emerged, water streaming from her dark hair, which hung down long enough to cover her shoulders but not her breasts.

She stared at him, wheezing desperately. Hands struggling to cover herself. He saw panic and embarrassment duelling for supremacy in her eyes. And he saw that – even in the open air – she couldn't breathe.

Her lips were a pale, unnatural blue.

Adrenaline rushed into Carter's veins.

He knew a panic attack when he saw one – he'd had them himself. He knew all too well the terrifying sensation of suffocation – the sense that all the oxygen had been drawn from the world, leaving none behind for him.

Kicking steadily to keep them both afloat, Carter tried to force her to meet his gaze.

"You're OK, Allie. Look at me." He kept his voice calm and authoritative, his eyes locked on hers. "Breathe slowly."

Allie thrashed in his grip and he shook his head sternly. "Don't look away." Her frightened grey eyes darted back to his. "Keep your eyes on me. Breathe slowly."

Wheezing audibly, she shook her head so violently cold water sprayed across his cheeks. She couldn't do it.

For the first time, Carter wondered if this wasn't a more serious situation than he'd thought. In the moonlight her face looked drained of colour. Her eyes were glassy.

He fought to stay calm. To keep his voice steady.

"Breathe in through your nose like this," he said, demonstrating. "And now out." He blew air out through his lips, forcefully.

She tried to do as he said – fighting for air, her eyes locked on his. But he could see it didn't work. Carter should have called for help earlier. He'd never seen anyone have a panic attack this bad. Then, to his horror, her eyelids fluttered shut, and her body went limp. She wasn't breathing.

There wasn't time to think. Holding her tight with one arm, he raised his free hand and slapped her cheek, hard. It physically hurt him to do it.

Her skin was like butter beneath the roughness of his hand. He felt like a monster.

Her eyes shot open. She took a sharp, reflexive breath.

Carter's heart leaped.

"You can do this, Allie," he said, believing it now. Willing her to believe. "Just breathe.'"

He took a deep breath, relief warming him when she tried to do the same, her gaze still locked on his, like he was the only person in the world.

"Good!" he said. "Again."

She took a deeper breath this time, and he could tell the panic was abating as oxygen filled her lungs, entering her blood stream. Her lips flushed with red.

"Again."

He'd been so focused on her breathing he hadn't noticed she was trembling until, on the fourth successful breath, she burst into tears.

"Carter…" she whispered brokenly.

That word told him everything. How embarrassed she was. How frightened.

He knew just what that felt like. Knew it far too well.

He didn't even think about what to do next. Without a word, he pulled her into his arms.

Ordinarily, he would never have dreamt of doing this. But there was nothing ordinary about this situation.

For a moment, he worried that she would reject his touch.

Instead, her arms tightened around his neck as she clung to him.

Just for a moment, he didn't think about her body pressed against his. Or about the fact that they were both naked and vulnerable. He thought only about protecting her. It was all he wanted. And he didn't know why.

"You're OK, Allie," he whispered. "Just keep breathing."

All around them, the laughter and splashing continued unabated. To the others, they must have looked like just another couple.

Still. He had to get her out of here.

But she seemed too stunned to make her own way. With one arm around her waist, he half-carried her to the shore.

Once they were on land, though, he stood uncertainly in the soft mud. They couldn't go back to the school like this.

"Where are your clothes?" he asked.

Here, in the open, he had to try very hard not to look at her. Allie, her arms crossed in front of her chest, was doing the same. Each of them stared just past the other's bare shoulder.

"I don't know," she admitted, shivering. "I can't remember where we left everything. It all just looks like … trees."

"Right," he said. "Plan B." He looked around, deciding what to do. "Stay here. I'll find something for you to wear."

Hurriedly, she turned to hide behind a cluster of trees. As she did, he glimpsed the pale curve of her hips. Long, smooth thighs.

It took all his strength to tear his gaze away.

Focus, Carter, he ordered himself. *Be a good guy.*

Taking a deep breath, he turned and headed into the forest, looking in the most obvious hiding places. Discarded clothing lay everywhere and he grabbed whatever looked useful.

Stones and pine cones bit into his bare feet like little knives as he hurried back to where he'd left his own clothing, pulling on his shorts and stuffing his sandy feet into his shoes. Then, still shirtless, he headed back to the cluster of trees.

The night air was cool against his bare shoulders.

At first he couldn't see her in the darkness, but then he nearly ran right into her. Suddenly, it was impossible to avoid seeing her – pale skin, curves, long dark hair. Grey, tormented eyes.

His heart stuttered.

He didn't trust himself to speak. Averting his gaze, he held out his own shirt and a pair of girl's shorts.

He hoped she couldn't see him well in the dark; his face was burning.

She grabbed the clothes from his hand and turned away. He could see her from the corner of his eye, bending to pull on the shorts.

The smooth line of her bare back was the most perfect thing he'd ever seen.

She fumbled with his T-shirt before she managed to yank it over her head.

An awkward silence fell. Carter cleared his throat to break it.

"Ready?" The word came out low, but reassuringly steady.

She nodded, eyes shining in the moonlight.

Cautiously, he held out his hand. She would swat it away, he thought. Or give him a withering look. But, instead, she took it without hesitation. Almost eagerly, as if she was glad he'd offered it.

Excitement flooded his veins with the dizzying force of a drug.

Something had changed between them tonight. For the first time, she trusted him.

And for the first time he was willing to admit he wanted her. In his life. In his clothes.

They walked across the forest towards the footpath, Allie picking her way carefully, feet still bare. He hadn't been able to find shoes.

They were leaving the lake now, the squeals and laughter of the summer splash fading with each step. After a few minutes, the only sound they could hear was their own breathing.

Carter relaxed a little. They'd done it. They'd escaped without anyone noticing.

When they reached the main path back to the school, Allie's steps slowed. She tugged at his hand until he stopped and looked down at her.

"Carter ... I just wanted to..." She hesitated, her eyes searching his face. "Thank you. You saved my life."

Reluctantly, he let go of her hand.

"It was nothing," he lied.

He knew it was the right thing to say. He had to pretend this was no big deal. He couldn't tell her the truth.

If she'd just let it go – let him get away with that small falsehood – maybe things would have been different. Maybe they could have kept pretending.

But she didn't.

"No, Carter." She grabbed his hand again, gripping it tightly.

Her gaze was so intense, the air left his lungs as he met it.

"It was something," she said.

Goosebumps ran across Carter's back. He stood very still. The moment seemed frozen in time. She'd nearly died tonight. They'd got through it together.

Everything was different now.

He longed to touch her cheek; to feel her skin, soft against his fingertips. He wanted to tell her he'd never felt closer to anyone than he felt to her right now. He wanted to tell her how beautiful she was. How strong.

He wanted to tell her the truth. Something in her expression told him she wanted to hear it.

But before he could summon the courage, a voice broke the spell.

"Allie!"

Jo raced up the path towards them. Gabe and Lisa were right behind her.

Allie turned towards them. As she did, her hand slipped free from Carter's hold.

Jo grabbed Allie by the shoulders and gave her a worried shake. "Where have you been? Are you OK? I looked for you everywhere."

Flushing guiltily, Allie started to explain, but Carter didn't wait to hear. He didn't want to see Jo shooting him an accusing look. Or have Gabe remind him, in that superior way of his, that Allie was Sylvain's girlfriend.

This was what was real. Not that moment with Allie's hand in his, or that look in her eyes. That was imaginary. He had to remember that.

With no one looking, Carter stepped back, and disappeared into the night.

That Scene in Carter's Room

Look, I know I made you wait a very long time for Allie and Carter's first kiss. I willingly admit this. But the build-up to this moment in Carter's room, when Allie comes to see him, ostensibly because she's furious about Katie but mostly because she just wants to see him, was so much fun to write.

I'd already written the kissing scenes with Allie and Sylvain earlier in the book, this wasn't my first ever make-out scene. And yet, it felt different to write. People often ask me how I knew who Allie would choose at the end of the series, and this scene was part of how I decided. Allie is surprised by how much she enjoys kissing Carter because I was surprised by how much she enjoyed it. I'd meant this to be a bit of an antidote to what happened with Sylvain, but it turned into much more. There is a visceral connection between them in this moment. The kiss *feels* right to both of them. There is a real connection. And a real connection is more than just enjoying a kiss. It's feeling part of something bigger than that. Something that might break your heart if it all goes wrong. It's like stepping off a cliff and trusting the other person will catch you. That takes a lot of trust. And it catches both of them off guard.

As I wrote this scene, I began to see the end of the book in my mind. I certainly knew who was going to win the first battle for Allie's heart, at any rate. For me, as for Allie, this moment mattered.

Here's the kissing scene in Carter's room, from his perspective.

When she smiled at him his heart jumped. When she laughed at his jokes his whole day improved.

Take a Chance

- CARTER -

Carter shut his bedroom window with a thump. He needed to concentrate – with everything that had been happening lately, he was miles behind on his class work. If he didn't catch up Zelazny would give him detention again. But it was after eleven and he'd only just now finished his essay on the War of the Roses.

There was so much left to do.

As he turned with weary resignation to his science assignment, the words swam on the page. Rubbing his eyes, he picked up his pen and frowned at the book in front of him. He was writing the first answer onto a clean sheet of paper when something – a tiny movement, or a subtle change in the light – made him look up.

A face – made unnaturally pale by the darkness – stared back at him from a place where nothing should be but sky.

With a startled cry he hurtled up and stumbled backward so fast his chair crashed to the floor.

Clinging to the window frame, Allie watched with obvious amusement.

In one quick glance, he took in the smooth lines of her oval face and her dark hair swirling in the breeze as she stood on the ledge outside his second-floor window. Her white cotton blouse hung loose from the skirt of her uniform. Her lips curled up at the corners, in the way they always did when she was about to laugh at him.

He strode over and unlatched the window.

"What the hell…?"

"I can't sleep," she whispered. "Want to come out and play?"

Her words made his heart trip but he kept his expression cynical. "You're mad. Get inside before you kill yourself."

She ducked down to climb through the arched, shutter-style window, her short-pleated skirt fluttering against her thighs. He pretended not to notice.

"Katie is such a *bitch*," she complained as she clambered across his desk.

"No argument."

As she told him what had happened that day, she paced his room like a panther in a cage. Watching her, Carter frowned. She was a bundle of nerves. Her hands flew and her shoes squeaked against the wood floor when she pivoted. Her voice was rich with righteous indignation and hurt.

When she described how Sylvain had intervened that morning with Katie and her friends, his muscles tensed. His hands curled into fists at his side.

What is it *with sodding Sylvain? Why is he always in the right place when she needs someone? How does he always manage to be the one?*

Suddenly, he was as stressed out as Allie. It felt weird to care so much.

If Carter was perfectly honest, he hadn't really liked her at first. He thought she knew more than she let on – that she was working some angle – a new girl pretending to be ordinary so she could get attention. A faker. But, over time, he'd started to believe she was who she said she was. Everything at Cimmeria seemed to blindside her. She did everything wrong. And her innocence made her vulnerable. So Katie and her friends bullied her and for a long time he'd thought Sylvain was doing the same. But now, he wasn't certain.

It wasn't like Sylvain to be so persistent.

But lately, his own feelings for Allie were confused. When she smiled at him his heart jumped. When she laughed at his jokes his whole day improved. He tried not to look at her amazing legs… Well. At least she'd never seen him looking.

The only problem was… They were friends. And if they became something else it would ruin their friendship forever. He wouldn't let that happen.

But she was looking up at him now, blinking those grey eyes that seemed to miss nothing; waiting for him to comment on all that had transpired on her first day as "School Murderer".

"Look," he said, "It seems to me there are only two possibilities. Either Katie didn't spread the first rumour and she's just taking advantage of it, or she *did* spread the first rumour and this is all part of her evil plan to get to you. Make people hate you."

She flinched a little at that.

"I think it's the latter," he concluded.

"What should we do?" She sat down on the edge of his bed, looking as comfortable as if she were in her own room. With a sigh, she stretched out her legs.

He wished she wouldn't do that.

"The rumours are intended to cause the most damage possible. This feels like a campaign to get rid of you."

Her cheeks flushed an angry red as she leaned forwards. "OK, Carter. Enough with secrecy and all that bollocks. It's time. Tell me about this place."

He didn't even have to think about it – he crossed his arms and set his jaw. "Allie, you know I can't—"

"Uh-uh." She cut him off. "Not this time. Someone *died*. For all I know, whoever killed Ruth could go after me next. You know things. You are allegedly my friend. You have to tell me."

When she got angry she had this way of tilting up her chin that was both adorable and threatening – she was doing it right now.

"I can't. If I did – and if anybody ever found out…" He shook his head. "I just can't – trust me."

"How can I trust you if you won't tell me the truth?" Under her breath she added, "Maybe I should just go ask Sylvain…"

That was too much.

The rush of anger and frustration left him seething. He stalked to where she sat and leaned over. He knew it was intimidating. He wanted to intimidate her. She needed to stop seeing Sylvain as an option – he wasn't good for her.

"Do you want to know what you mean to Sylvain? Well, I'll tell you. Every year he picks a pretty new first-year girl, shags her and dumps her. It's his thing." So, he was exaggerating – Sylvain didn't *exactly* do that. But he came close to it. And she needed to stay away from him. "Each one thinks she's *so* special. That's who you are to him, Allie. His newest, naive conquest."

"Stop it!" The colour drained from her cheeks and she shoved him hard, jumping to her feet. "If that's true, why didn't you ever tell me before, Carter?"

She stood, practically touching him. Searching his face as if she could find all the answers there.

He stuttered. "I … I … I tried."

But she wasn't letting him off that easily. "People say you're into one night stands. So... How are you any different than Sylvain?"

That stung. "Are these the same people who say you killed Ruth?"

"Whatever." She tilted her head to one side. Judging him. "Are they lying about you?"

What could he say? Yes … and no. His thoughts flickered back to Clare's tear-stained face after he broke up with her last term. The way her friends had circled her.

"Yes, Allie," he said with more confidence than he felt. "It's a lie. Or at least an exaggeration. Look. I got this… I guess, reputation … because if I go out with someone and I can tell they're not the right one for me I break up with them right away. I don't want to hurt anybody, Allie. I really don't. It's just, sometimes…"

His voice trailed off. *God, I sound so lame.*

A long moment passed as she held his gaze. He waited for her to laugh, or shake her head in disgust. But she didn't move. She was so close he could see the tiny flecks of dark blue in the grey of her eyes, and the way her dark eyelashes curled up at the very ends.

Then, to his surprise, she held up her hand.

"OK." Her voice was soft, words like feathers against his skin. "I believe you."

Her light scent danced on the air between them. For a second, he closed his eyes – breathed it in. Why was she standing so *close*?

Walk away, Carter, he told himself. *Don't mess this up.*

Instead, as if someone else controlled his body, he pressed his palm against hers. The warmth of her skin startled him like an electric charge.

"Thank you," he heard himself say. *Shut up, Carter,* he thought frantically.

"For what?" Her voice sounded small.

"For believing me."

Her lips quirked up and his eyes were drawn to them. The muscles in his throat constricted. His fingers entwined with hers.

This is such a bad idea…

He said something – he wasn't sure what. Just anything that would keep her here, holding his hand.

She said something back but all he could hear was the roar of blood rushing through his veins as he pulled her towards him. Now she was so close, he could feel her breath soft and warm against his face. She smelled like peppermint and honeysuckle. It made him dizzy.

From here, kissing her was easy – all he had to do was lean forwards.

When his lips touched hers she gave a little gasp of surprise. For a second he was so certain she'd pull away he almost let go of her. But then she reached her hands up to his neck and pulled him closer.

Relief flooded over him like cool water as he tightened his arms around her shoulders.

"I've waited so long for this," he whispered.

In reply, her lips parted and she pressed her fingertips hard into the muscles of his back. He tasted the faint salt of her mouth against his tongue as his hands knotted in the fabric of her uniform. He crushed her in his arms.

She was so warm – his body felt hot wherever it touched her. Carter's head swam as he clung to her. He wanted to pull her so close she could never escape. He wanted to feel her body pressed against his forever.

Slipping his lips across her jaw to her neck, he moved downy tendrils of hair aside to reach the skin behind her ear. When he pressed his teeth against the tender flesh of her earlobe she made a soft sound and his entire body responded – his breath shortened and his heart thudded as if it were trying to escape from his chest.

She was so soft against his body. Soft, but strong and eager – her fingers tangled in his hair as she pulled his mouth back to hers. He could get lost in this so easily. Lost in her. Forget about all the awful things that had happened and just think about *this*. Nobody knew they were together. Nobody was going to walk in on them. And something told him that for whatever reason – maybe for all the wrong reasons – she wasn't going to be the one to step back.

But one thing held him back. This was Allie.

He had to be careful. It would be so easy to screw things up now. To go too far and ruin it all. To lose her.

To lose everything.

Cupping her face in his hands, he kissed her one last time. Then, regretfully, he extracted himself from her arms and backed up until he leaned against the cool wall by the door, where he tried to calm his rapid breathing and stop himself from running back to scoop her up and carry her to his bed, which was *right there*.

She stayed frozen where he'd left her, a worried gaze locked on his.

He held out his hands. "I hate to do the grown-up thing, but…"

What had happened between them seemed to have lowered her defences – for a brief moment her every emotion was written clearly on her face. At first she looked confused. Then colour stained her cheeks and he knew she was embarrassed.

Holding her gaze steadily, he waited for her to understand that he wasn't rejecting her. He knew she would. She could always read him like a book.

And after a long second she did. Then she smiled a knowing smile so beautiful she seemed to glow.

"So," she said. "What do we do now?"

Carter and Jules

The course of true love never does run smoothly, and that is certainly true of Carter and Allie. Nearly as quickly as they get together, they fall apart again. And while Allie considers choosing Sylvain instead, Carter is drawn to his old friend Jules.

This was tricky to write. It's hard to make characters sympathetic if they are so easily moving on to someone else. But it felt very real to me. In any relationship at any time, it can be hard to be certain you've made the right choice. There are so many directions our lives can take, especially when we're young, it always felt true that Carter and Allie would struggle to be certain of one another.

And there is something about old friends that makes us feel safe. I have this feeling that, if he never met Allie, Carter might have ended up with Jules. It wouldn't have lasted but at Cimmeria, they could have been a golden couple. Then Allie came along with her feistiness and her messed-up family, and he forgot all about Jules.

But Jules never forgot him.

In real life, I suspect Jules would have loved him more than he loved her. And that would have left him conflicted. So in this scene where we get to see the two of them together, dealing with their emotional differences, and finding their way through this new minefield of a relationship. I wanted to explore the dynamics of that relationship — his ambivalence, and her confidence.

Want to know the worst thing about it? I kind of liked them as a couple. He brought out the best in Jules, and she kept him focussed. But we don't always make decisions about love with logic. We make them with our hearts. A lesson they are both about to learn.

Here's Carter with Jules, the night of the Winter Ball.

Tonight, though,

everything seemed

different. She seemed

different.

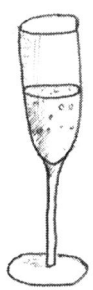

The Winter Ball
– CARTER –

"Where the bloody hell is that shoe? Waste of sodding time ..."

Grumbling to himself, Carter crouched down to search the back of his wardrobe, throwing out trainers, boots and a scarf he didn't recognise before finally emerging a minute later, black dress shoes firmly in one hand.

His tuxedo jacket hung from the back of the wardrobe door, black as his mood.

The idea of going to the winter ball right now, given all that was happening, seemed patently absurd. Isabelle should have cancelled it.

The possibility of some sort of an attack was too high. And after what happened at the summer ball...

He sighed. The party was happening and there was no getting out of it.

He dressed quickly, clipping the cuffs of his crisp, white shirt with the cufflinks Bob Ellison had given to him on his sixteenth birthday – or rather, passed on. Made of silver with a faceted garnet stone at the centre, they'd once belonged to his father. But Carter had long since given up examining the cold metal for any connection to his dead parents. There was nothing there.

They were just cufflinks.

He stood in front of the mirror, knotting his black tie with the expert ease of familiarity. For a moment he studied himself, seeing the irritation in his dark eyes. The tight set of his full mouth.

He clenched and unclenched his hands, trying to force himself to relax.

It was nearly nine o'clock. He'd put this off for as long as he could.

* * *

The sound of the party hit him at the top of the stairs. In the great hall, a string orchestra played a lively waltz. The roar of conversation rose above the music like a wave cresting over a beach.

Squaring his shoulders, Carter walked into the crowds.

He would show his face, hang out with Jules for a bit then leave when no one was looking. That was enough.

The ground floor was packed with elegantly dressed strangers and Carter struggled to make his way through them, forcing a polite smile.

A familiar voice broke above the others and he saw Jules, reaching out through the crush of people.

"Carter's trapped! I'll rescue him," she announced, grabbing his hand and pulling him through to where she stood talking to Katie and some of her vile acolytes.

Katie cast a bored smile his way. She looked white as milk in a dark green dress that clung to her figure but he barely noticed her. Because Jules looked *incredible*.

Her black, silk dress slid over her body like dark water. A slit from the ankle to the thigh exposed one muscular leg. Her silky blonde hair just brushed the very tops of her mostly bare shoulders.

"Blimey, Jules. You look fantastic," he said, trying not to stare.

She blushed. "You scrub up pretty well yourself, Carter."

Her words slurred slightly. He could smell the wine on her breath. His lips quirked up. "Why, Miss Matheson. Have you been drinking?"

"Only champagne." She blinked. "That doesn't count ... does it?"

"Not if I have some." He lifted two glasses from a passing tray held aloft by a hassled waiter and handed one to her. "If we must be here, the least we can do is get drunk."

"Intoxicated is the correct term." Katie took a sip from her glass and eyed a couple of glamorous adults nearby. "Drunk is what ordinary people get."

'And we're not ordinary,' her friend Ismay snickered next to her.

Carter followed Katie's gaze and recognised the older couple as Sylvain's parents.

Jules didn't miss his expression.

"Shall we dance?" She tilted her head to one side and looked at him thoughtfully as if merely considering this possibility. Then she made up her mind. "Yes. We shall."

Without waiting for his response, she pulled him to the edge of the crowded dance floor. Carter, who didn't want to dance but also didn't want to talk to Katie, upended his champagne glass, downing its contents. Jules did the same.

Setting their glasses on a nearby table, Carter turned to her, taking her hand in his, and resting his other hand on her waist. She was more muscular than Allie, he noticed. And taller.

He winced. He really needed to stop comparing them.

Setting his mouth in a determined line he pulled her closer. They swirled into the crowd.

They'd known each other since they were eleven. They'd learned to fight together. To dance together. And it showed. Jules seemed to anticipate his every move. She let him lead without question or challenge. He imagined dancing with Allie would be very different.

She'd never let anyone lead.

I have got to stop thinking about her.

As they spun across the floor, he pulled her closer, flattening his hand against the small of her back. Beneath his fingers she moved with sinuous ease.

Her gaze held his as if she willed him to think only of her. The way her body pressed against his made it hard to think about anything else.

Carter swallowed hard. He'd never thought of Jules as anything but a friend. Tonight, though, everything seemed different. *She* seemed different.

She was openly flirting with him, for one thing.

When the song finished she raised her lips to his ear. "Let's get more champagne."

Her words seemed to run from his head down his spine.

He looked into her dark blue eyes. Maybe he *could* forget Allie.

She led him to the edge of the dance floor, waving over a waiter bearing a tray full of champagne glasses. Selecting two, she handed one to Carter.

He knew he should pace himself but the cold, effervescent wine was welcome. The room was stuffy. Over-heated.

Jules took a deep drink then turned to face him. She was standing very close and her breast brushed his arm.

Just for a second, he wondered if she'd done it on purpose.

"I'm so glad I don't have to wear a jacket like boys do." Her voice was husky. "It must be so hot."

Somehow, his glass of champagne was empty again. *When did that happen?*

His hand, of its own accord, ran down her bare arm. Her skin felt as silky as her dress. When it reached her wrist he pulled her closer.

Is this a good idea? But the cautious voice came and went away.

Her lips were so near now. Her body was pressed against his. He could feel how her breaths had shortened. The way her pulse fluttered. She wanted him as much as he wanted her. And why shouldn't they have each other? Should he just be alone forever because he and Allie couldn't make it work? Because she wanted someone else?

Because she wanted Sylvain?

No.

"Carter..." Jules whispered.

"What?" His throat had tightened.

People were pushing past them to the dance floor, but they barely noticed.

"Are you ever going to kiss me?" she asked.

He smiled, and lowered his lips to hers.

At first, all he noticed was how different it was with her than Allie. Jules smelled differently – of cool roses rather than honeysuckle and spice. Her body felt different. But it was more than that. Her kisses were more assured. Allie was always hesitant, curious, as if she was still learning how to do it. Jules, on the other hand, was confident. Her lips parted instantly, explored him. Her tongue brushed against his. Her hands slipped under his jacket and ran up his back, pulling him tighter.

Things went faster with Jules. Got out of hand faster. And, after a moment he pulled back, half-laughing.

"Hey, we better chill out a little. Parents."

Her lips curved up. "I know a place we can go where there aren't any parents."

He held her gaze. "Where?"

"My room."

The noise of the crowd seemed to recede. Carter's heartbeat sped up. He wanted nothing more right now than to continue that kiss. But he knew if that happened – if he went to her room and they continued what they'd started at the edge of the dance floor – their friendship would change forever.

He hesitated. "I don't know…"

Her face fell.

With a gentle touch, he smoothed a strand of blonde hair back from her eyes. "Are you sure about this, Jules? We've always been friends."

She took a quick breath. When she spoke, her words came out in a rush. "I am sure, Carter. I've been sure for a long time. I just didn't know how to tell you. Then you were with Allie and I thought…"

His face darkened. *You thought it was forever. Well, so did I. And look how wrong we both were.*

That made up his mind. He pressed a soft kiss against the side of her face.

"Let's go."

Jules smiled and took charge. "I'll go up now. You wait five minutes then follow me. It wouldn't be good for people to see us going up the stairs together. They won't notice us apart."

Boys weren't allowed in the girls' dorm but Jules was a prefect. She knew how to get around The Rules better than anyone.

After she'd disappeared into the crowd, Carter grabbed another glass of champagne and strolled around the room. Five minutes seemed to take forever to pass.

Now that he'd made up his mind he wanted to be there. With her.

Nearby, Sylvain had joined his parents – Carter's gaze flitted past them to the dance floor. As he watched, Jo swirled by in a sexy velvet mini-dress only she could carry off. She'd dyed her hair bright pink.

Just looking at her made Carter smile. Jo was like human sunshine. He'd have to remember to tell her later how cool she looked.

Allie was nowhere to be seen, and he was glad.

Maybe she hadn't come. He knew she'd tried to get Isabelle to cancel the whole event.

Turning, he weaved a little, stumbling against a chair before he caught himself. He was starting to feel lightheaded – he hadn't eaten anything since lunch and had just had … how many glasses of champagne?

He needed food.

With effort, he made his way through the throngs to the space where tables were piled high. Without really looking at what he chose, he filled a plate with hors d'oeuvres.

Leaning against a wall he ate quickly, watching the dance from a safe distance.

He'd been part of Cimmeria all his life – had hidden at the top of the stairs as a small boy to watch the glamorous set below – but never felt a true part of events like these. With no parents to accompany him, no connection to these people at all aside from Cimmeria itself, he was at once one of them and nothing like them at all.

When he finished, he set the empty plate down on a passing waiter's tray and glanced at his watch. Time to go.

A lock of dark hair fell forwards and he pushed it back as he lifted himself from the wall.

That was when he saw her.

In a dark blue dress that perfectly suited her figure, Allie moved slowly through the crowd like a disconsolate starlet. Her hair poured in vivid red waves down her back.

She stood out like a warning light.

Carter's heart seemed to stop.

She and Jo must have coloured their hair together. But, while Jo had seemed giddy, Allie looked pale and unhappy.

He fought an instinctive urge to go to her, to find out what was wrong. To fix it.

She wasn't his to fix anymore. And besides, Jules was waiting...

As Allie neared him though, he didn't move. He could have slipped away without her ever seeing him. But he stood there.

Despite everything, he still felt drawn to her. Something connected them. She was the only person he knew here who was like him – an outsider. The only one who really got him. Even though he was still angry and hurt, he also missed having her in his life.

She was so close now he could almost touch her but she hadn't noticed him yet. Like a ghost, he watched unseen as she picked up a canapé, studied it then put it in her mouth cautiously.

Something about the way she did that, the innocence of it, made up his mind.

He moved closer. He'd almost reached her side when she turned suddenly into him.

"I'm sorr—" The words died on each of their lips as they bumped into each other.

"Allie..." He couldn't seem to talk. To think.

Their eyes locked. Colour flooded her pale cheeks. For a moment that stretched too long, neither of them said anything. Finally, Carter opened his mouth to tell her how lovely she looked. Just as he did she turned away with a jerk, as if she wanted to escape. As if she couldn't bear even to *look* at him.

Despair ran like ice water through his veins. How had they managed to ruin everything so completely?

Without another word, he fled. He had to stop fooling himself that anything could be resurrected between them. That they could ever be together again.

He had to let her go.

Weaving through the crowd he ran up the stairs, taking them two at a time.

But when he knocked on Jules' door seconds later, his hand quivered. He tightened it into a fist.

Jules opened the door immediately. "Bad news," she said. "We can't stay long. Isabelle wants me downstairs for speeches. We have ten minutes."

With that, she grabbed his lapel and pulled him into the room.

Carter almost smiled. Jules was so uninhibited. So sure of what she wanted. Maybe this was what he needed now in his life. Something uncomplicated.

Someone uncomplicated.

He closed the door, leaning his back against it as he looked around.

Her room smelled faintly of her perfume. One wall held a framed poster of an old man with a guitar all painted in dark blue hues. A soft, white rug covered the floor. The bookshelves were stacked with photos, books and knick-knacks. It felt comfortable.

She'd draped a scarf over the bedside lamp, giving it all an ethereal glow. The scarf fluttered in the breeze coming through the open window. The icy air felt good – cooling the perspiration on his skin.

It occurred to him it was cold enough to snow.

She took a step towards him. Her skin glowed in the light.

"Listen, Jules …" He faltered and she looked at him with concern.

"What's the matter? Did something happen?"

"I just think…" He reached for her hand, threading his fingers through hers. "We need to be careful. You matter to me. And I couldn't bear to lose you. After Allie, I'm afraid that…" He shook his head. "I'm afraid."

"Shhh." Reaching up, she rested her palm gently against his face. His eyes drifted shut as he leaned in to her touch.

He'd been so lonely for so long it hurt not to be alone.

"Listen to me, Carter West," she said with soft determination. "You will *never* lose me. Whatever happens tonight or tomorrow night or all the tomorrows after, I will always be there for you. Do you understand me? Always."

As she said the words he'd always wanted Allie to say his eyes flew open. He saw nothing in her dark blue gaze but love and honesty.

He so wanted to believe she was right. Maybe, all this time, he'd been looking in the wrong place. Trying to make something happen with Allie when Jules was right here. Waiting for him.

"Jules…" With a sigh of surrender he lowered his lips to hers.

* * *

Twenty minutes later, Carter and Jules walked down a side staircase to the ground floor, hand-in-hand. He could still feel the touch of her lips against his. Smell her scent on his clothes. They moved with easy synchronisation.

He felt happy for the first time in weeks. His thoughts were clear of the haze that had hung over them since he and Allie had broken up. He felt focussed. Alive.

As they neared the great hall, Carter noticed the crowds seemed to have thinned. Jules looked around with a puzzled frown.

"I hope we haven't missed the speeches." Dropping his hand, she hurried her pace. "Isabelle will kill me."

Before he could reply, they both heard the pounding of footsteps. A Night School student shot by them, loosening his tie as he ran. He was heading for the basement staircase.

Someone called their names.

Everything seemed to move in slow motion as they turned in unison to see Zelazny sprinting down the wide hallway towards them.

"Training Room," the instructor said without breaking stride. "Now."

Carter and Jules exchanged a tense look.

Jules spoke first. "I guess the party's over."

Sylvain at the Winter Ball

Hoo, boy. Sylvain at the Winter Ball. Filled with frustration and love and confusion and passion — a bundle of sexy energy, wrapped up in a very attractive package. Goodness me.

I hate to admit this, because I know some of you will disagree, but I loved Sylvain and Allie. Not early in book one when he's a selfish git, but later when he begins to realise that actions have consequences, and that Allie has agency and he can't control her. Then, when he begins to grow up and see her as a full human being with strength and independence, he becomes kind of amazing. His character arc, from entitled, spoiled brat to trustworthy warrior-friend, is one of my favourite parts of the series.

And have no doubt of this: He loves Allie. This is real, clear-eyes, full-heart, can't-lose *love*. The kind of love you never get over. The kind that ten years later, when you're all grown up with a car and an apartment in the city and a job, still hurts, just a little.

I didn't realise the full depth of his emotion for her until I wrote this chapter. For Allie, it's not exactly the same. Not yet anyway. She's being a little selfish in this scene — taking what she wants. She's confused and lost and Sylvain adores her, and it is incredibly nice to be adored. She does come to love him later, in her own way. But in this scene at the Winter Ball, she's spreading her wings, and testing her power. Wondering if she kisses him will he fall in love with her? And the answer to that question is: yes. But she's playing with fire. His true love means that he is vulnerable and so could she. They could both get badly hurt.

But she doesn't realise that yet. This moment is all about the heady exploration of lust and emotion and connection. And who better to explore that with than Sylvain Cassel? Nobody, I say.

Here's the kiss at the Winter Ball from Sylvain's point of view.

Then the silence

returned again, so

heavy with unspoken

words it seemed to

weigh them both

down.

We Can Take It Back

– SYLVAIN –

Sylvain Cassel stared across the crowded ballroom, his parents' voices fading into the background. A glass of champagne lingered forgotten in one hand. The music swirling around him had an almost physical force, but he barely noticed.

On the other side of the hall, a flame-haired girl in a vintage blue dress threaded her way with unconscious grace through the well-dressed throng.

He couldn't take his eyes off her. He'd never seen Allie look as beautiful as she did tonight.

"Sylvain, *mon cher*, have we lost you?"

His mother's amused voice dragged him out of his reverie.

He glanced up to find both his parents watching him with undisguised merriment. His mother, gorgeous as ever in a couture silk gown; his father suave and relaxed in a perfectly cut Hugo Boss tuxedo exactly like the one Sylvain wore.

He didn't like the way they were looking at him now, though. As if he was a child.

"I'm sorry," he said stiffly. "What were you saying?"

They resumed their conversation about his Uncle Henri's new yacht, and how absurd it was that he'd acquired another.

For a minute, Sylvain feigned interest, but his gaze was drawn towards Allie's retreating back.

He didn't want to be here right now, making polite conversation with his parents.

He wanted to be with her.

Abruptly setting his half-empty glass down on a tray carried by a passing waiter, he leaned forwards to interrupt his parents' conversation.

"Désolé, Maman, Papa," he said. "Would you mind if I left you for just a moment?"

His mother inclined her head, her gaze knowing.

His father's expression, though, was cautious. He reached for Sylvain's arm.

"*Cherche ta fille,*" he said in French, his voice low. *Find your girl.* "But be careful. She is no ordinary girl."

A frown creased Sylvain's brow. He pulled his arm free of his father's hand. "I'm always careful."

He didn't linger to ask what his father meant but, as he walked into the crowd, Sylvain couldn't get his words out of his head.

No ordinary girl? What did that mean? Because she was Lucinda Meldrum's granddaughter? Or because she was Nathaniel's target?

Either way, it didn't matter – Sylvain was in love with Allie Sheridan. He had been for so long he could no longer remember a time when she wasn't the first thing he thought about in the morning. Or when hers wasn't the first face he sought in any room.

And yet she had never loved him.

But maybe now…

The possibility – the slight chance – that things had changed between them, made his heart stutter. He'd seen something in her eyes when she'd looked at him tonight – a new openness. A new warmth.

Had she finally forgiven him? Did he have a chance?

He weaved his way around clusters of men in tuxedos and women in expensive ball gowns, barely glancing at them. The crowded ballroom was stuffy, and he loosened his black tie just a little as he walked out the door of the great hall.

The elegant crowd had spilled out of the ballroom into the wide, formal hallway, and it was impossible to see beyond them. Sylvain climbed a few steps up the curved staircase to look for Allie, leaning over the heavy bannister to get a view.

There. At the end of the wide, expanse of hallway – its polished oak panelling gleaming in the light of the chandelier – he spotted a flash of bright red.

Sylvain couldn't suppress a smile. What had she done to her hair? It had been its usual golden-brown the last time he'd seen her.

Jo must have had something to do with it – her hair was the most extraordinary shade of pink all of a sudden.

It was good to see the two of them being friends again. He knew their falling out had hurt them both.

In the distance, Allie slowed her pace and looked around, as if deciding what to do. Then, with sudden determination, she pulled open the heavy front door and slipped out into the night.

Sylvain frowned. It was freezing out there. Snow was predicted. And she was wearing nothing more than a silk frock and a pair of fragile heels.

Something was up.

Swinging over the bannister, he leaped from the staircase to the floor in a single, balletic movement, landing lightly on the balls of his feet.

A nearby cluster of party goers murmured in surprise and swayed away from him.

"Sorry," he said with a quick, unapologetic smile.

Then, he ran down the hallway, and followed Allie out through the school's front door.

The cold took his breath away. It was a deep, threatening cold that turned each breath into a cloud, and rendered his fingertips instantly numb.

He pulled his tuxedo jacket more snugly across his shoulders and looked around.

Allie must be freezing out here.

Standing on the top step, he peered into the darkness. The curved drive was lined with Bentleys and Rolls Royces parked bumper-to-bumper and glistening like oil. A group of drivers had gathered by one of them, drinking steaming tea from thermoses and talking quietly.

On instinct, Sylvain turned to his left, staring intently at the dark edge of the woods.

Then he saw it. A flicker of movement. A low tree branch swaying, as if someone had just pushed it aside.

Excitement fluttered in his stomach. He knew where Allie was headed: the folly.

Leaping from the top step to the cold, hard ground, he ran after her, his calf-skin dress shoes skidding just a little. His heart beat out a cadence of hope as he turned onto the footpath.

The folly. Where he'd taught her to fight.

The folly. Where she'd first begun to doubt Carter.

There was something about that domed marble gazebo hidden in the trees that drew them to each other. It was their place.

And no matter how much she might have wanted to deny that fact, he knew Allie was aware of it, too.

Overhead, the sky was soft, grey velvet. Clouds, heavy with snow, absorbed all sound. The school grounds were silent and empty.

A huge party was taking place five minutes' walk away but, as he followed Allie's footsteps, Sylvain felt as if the two of them had the world all to themselves.

She was close now – he could almost feel her presence.

His heart thudding painfully, he pushed a low, overhanging branch aside and stepped into the clearing.

She was standing near the foot of the marble steps leading up to the folly. Her back was to him.

He watched as she reached out one tentative hand and rested it against the structure's cold Italian stone.

Her skin was luminescent against the midnight backdrop of her dress. She looked like a statue. Like a goddess. He could see the side of her face, the curve of her pale cheek beneath that torrent of glossy red hair.

Suddenly, he couldn't breathe.

Had he ever wanted anyone as much as he wanted her now?

Never.

He took a slow steadying breath. He had to play this right. He needed her to know she could trust him. He needed her to come to him.

"You're not wearing a coat, you know."

As soon as the words were out of his mouth, he wanted to take them back. Everyone thought he was so sophisticated. He'd had the entire night to think of what to say, and that was what he'd come up with?

For a moment she didn't react. Then, with aching slowness, she turned to face him.

Her expression was serious – almost sad – as her eyes met his. Those eyes. They were exactly the same colour as the storm clouds above them.

"Neither are you." Her voice was low. Disturbingly steady.

At that moment, it took everything in Sylvain not to run to her and crush her in his arms.

Instead, he unbuttoned his tuxedo, affecting absolute cool.

"True. But I at least have this." He shrugged his black, silk-lined jacket off and held it out to her.

For the first time, the hint of a smile curved the corners of her lips.

"But now you'll be cold," she said.

"I'll live."

For a brief second, he thought she might refuse. But then she reached out and took the jacket, draping it over her shoulders.

Now, he could fool himself that she was his.

"Thank you."

There was something still about her – as if she were waiting for something.

"You've changed your hair." His gaze traced the vivid curls over her shoulders. "It suits you."

Her hand rose to touch a curl. "It wasn't my idea. Jo can be . . . convincing."

Sylvain had to smile.

"So, I've heard." An awkward silence fell, and he tried to think of safe subjects to discuss.

"I'm sorry about my parents," he said quickly. "They just really wanted to meet you."

Her responding shrug was expressive. She knew all about parents.

"Your mum is gorgeous," she said, relaxing a little. "Like a movie star."

Fully aware of how much his mother would like knowing she thought this, Sylvain gave a wry smile. "I'll tell her you said so."

Then the silence returned again, so heavy it seemed to weigh them both down.

Allie shifted her weight on to one delicate sandal, digging the toe of the other into the dirt. He could sense her nervous anticipation. She was waiting for something.

He leaned against a stone pillar, eyes never leaving her.

His throat was so tight now. When he spoke, his voice was barely above a whisper.

"What are you doing out in the cold, Allie?"

He saw her quick intake of nervous breath. "I don't know . . . I guess I just needed some air." Her eyes challenged him. "What are you doing out here?"

There were so many things he could have said. So many lies he could have told. But he would never lie to her. So, he told her the truth.

"I followed you."

All the colour left her face. She was as pale as the marble folly next to her. As white as the statue of the dancing girl inside.

"Why?" She breathed the word.

Again, a thousand lies hung just out of his reach.

"*Le coeur a ses raisons que la raison ne connaît point.*" He recited the French phrase he'd learned only a few weeks ago, knowing she wouldn't understand. Knowing it would upset her not to. But never had a sentence summed up how he felt so completely.

The heart has reasons that reason cannot know.

Allie flushed. "What does that mean?"

He held her gaze with his. It was time to be brave.

He took a deep, icy cold breath. "It means that I want to be with you. That I can't get you out of my head." He pounded his fist with restrained violence against the pillar next to him. "I have tried everything I know to try, and you're still there."

Allie was visibly trembling now. She lifted one shaking hand as if to touch her forehead and then dropped it again.

"I think about you, too.' He could barely hear her over the thudding of his heart. 'But…"

He saw the look in her eyes. The doubt.

He felt the heat rise to his face. That night. That awful, horrible, stupid night.

In a flash, he remembered the fear in her eyes. The way she'd struggled against him. The confusion and hurt in her face.

Say you want me, he'd whispered to her. Wanting to humiliate her. To punish her for the power she held over him. Intending to push her away from him forever.

And he had succeeded. For she had never forgiven him.

God, he loathed himself for that night. That single minute in time. For the awful, selfish bastard he had been then.

He had to stop himself from doubling over, his heart hurt that much.

Could they never put it behind them? Would she never forgive him for who he used to be?

And worst of all, should she forgive him? Were some things simply unforgiveable?

But he had to try. He had to at least do that. He had to make her understand that he wasn't that person anymore. That he hated that person. And that he loved her.

For a moment he closed his eyes, willing the pain away. Then he looked at her again.

"I know I did a bad thing. A stupid, awful thing. But people change, Allie." His voice was passionate, almost desperate. "People learn. If they didn't, what would be the point of this?" His arm swept towards the school building they could just make out through the trees. "What would be the point of life? You've changed while you've been here – I've watched you change. Well, I've changed too. And I'm sorry about what I did that night. If there was some way to take it all back . . . I would give anything."

His voice broke and he turned away, a hand covering his eyes.

It was pointless. She hated him and she always would. And that was as it should be. It was all he deserved.

He stepped back, intending to flee. Then she took a gasping breath and stepped towards him.

Surprised, he looked up to find her extraordinary grey eyes ablaze with determination.

"You can take it back," she said. "You can."

Sylvain stared at her – too surprised to speak, too shocked to move as Allie ran across the space that divided them. His jacket slid from her shoulders, pooling forgotten on the frosty ground.

Then she was in front of him, hands reaching up to touch his face. Cold fingers stroking his skin. "Let's just take it all back."

Sylvain, who had dreamed of this moment for months, couldn't believe it was really happening. But her hands were real.

She was close to him now. He could feel the warmth of her breath on his skin. Smell the faint, honeysuckle scent of her shampoo.

Then, standing on her toes, she pressed her lips against his, and pulled him down towards her.

Her lips were soft and warm. He could taste the salt of her tears. She was real. This was real.

As if he was waking from a dream, Sylvain moved with slow caution, sliding his hands across the silk of her dress and pulling her into the warmth of his arms.

She leaned into him and the kiss grew more confident, more assured.

With his tongue, he brushed the edge of her lips. When her lips parted for him instantly, he groaned softly at the back of his throat. Her lips were gentle but insistent. He knew now she had been longing, too.

His bones seemed to soften as he pulled her closer to him. She was so close now, he could feel her heart skipping with uneven excitement. Her breasts were soft against his chest Everything about her was warm and wonderful. If it were possible to drown in a person he was drowning in her now. She kissed him with a pent-up passion that reflected his own, reaching up to tangle her fingers in his hair.

He knew as well as he knew anything that she was forgiving him. Accepting him.

Choosing him.

He was the one she wanted. Only him. At last.

Murmuring words in French, Sylvain brushed kisses on her cold cheeks, and the delicate skin of her eyes, the soft hair that framed her face. He breathed in her scent like oxygen.

Then their lips met again, hungry for more.

He could feel the heat of her body through the thin silk of her dress as she pressed herself against him, pulling him so close he was afraid he would hurt her. He couldn't breathe but he didn't care. He never wanted to breathe again.

He wanted to die right here, right now. Breathless and in love.

His lips moved down the side of her face to her ear then on to her neck and, breathing in short gasps, she dropped her head back.

Then, with a small cry that startled him, she straightened in his arms. "Sylvain, look! It's snowing!"

Reluctant to let her out of his reach, he held her close and looked up into the infinity of snow falling from a night sky before glancing back at her. Snowflakes had settled on her red hair where they glistened like diamonds. Her eyes were filled with wonder.

God, he loved her.

"It's a sign," he said, pressing his lips against her cheek. "A sign that we belong together."

The snow fell around them, thick and fast. Sylvain's blood sang with exhilaration. He barely noticed that she never replied.

Sylvain's Fight with Gabe

The fight involving Sylvain, Gabe, and Allie in *Legacy* is the pivotal moment in the series for me. So *much* happens in this chapter! Allie betrays Carter and Isabelle by not telling them her plans. She risks her life and Sylvain's life to speak with her brother, whom she really should not trust. Sylvain agrees to go with her and is nearly killed when the two of them are sabotaged by Gabe. The bond between Allie and Sylvain is made real and solid when they risk everything for each other. It is a bond that will never go away, no matter what happens in their lives from then on. So this fight matters.

I have to admit, I love writing fight scenes. The author Cassandra Clare once said that writing fight scenes is similar to writing kissing scenes because you have to be aware constantly of where everyone's hands are, and how they're moving, and what everyone is thinking. Also, everything has to make sense or readers will get lost. When I'm writing, I find I have to 'see' a fight scene in my head — I need to watch it play like a film. If I can visualise it, I can write it more believably.

Sometimes I actually act it out at my computer, punching the air like a boxer. I must look like a complete idiot. This is why there's tape over my computer camera lens. Nobody can ever see this.

Anyway.

In this scene, Allie is hiding while Gabe very nearly kills Sylvain. For endless minutes, Sylvain is on his own being used as a punching bag by a psychopath. This is a long way from the private jets and manor houses that have dominated his life until now. Now, it's all about survival.

Here's the fight in the woods from Sylvain's perspective.

Hate filled him with cold clarity. Hate enhanced his senses and helped him move with stealth and speed. Hate gave him purpose.

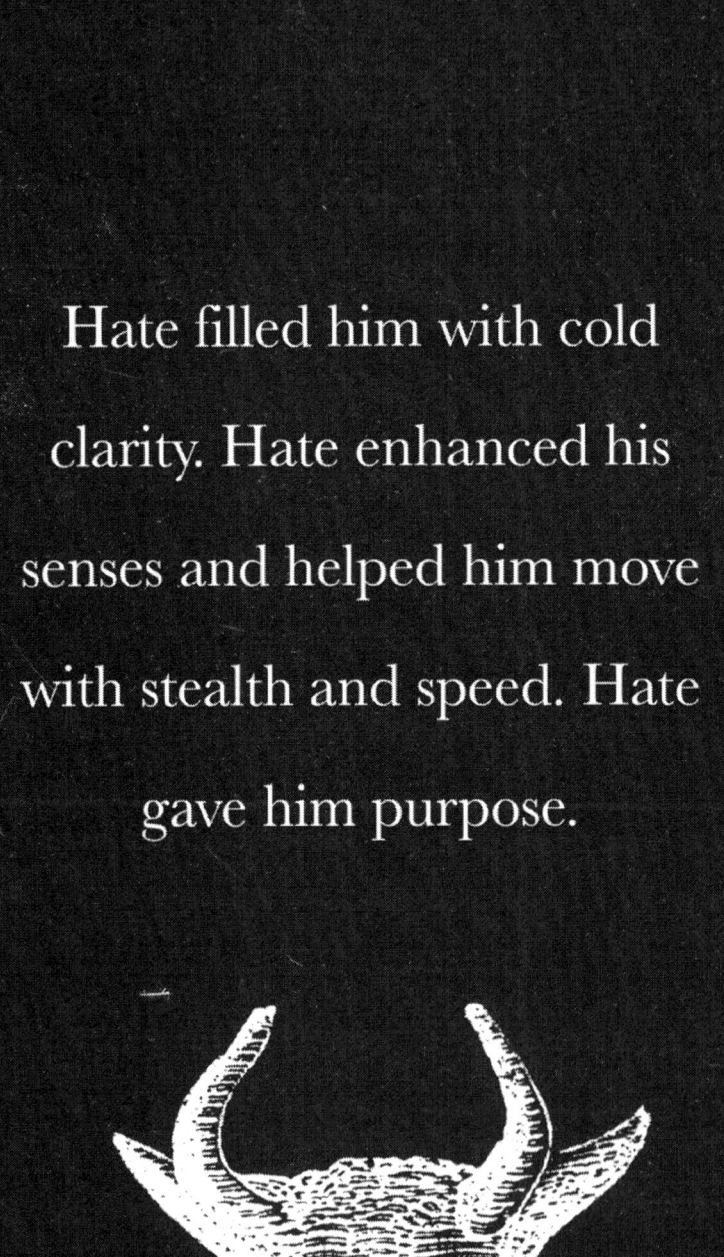

We Need to Run

– SYLVAIN –

Crouched low amid the bracken, Sylvain stared out through a thick curtain of trees. In the distance, Cimmeria Academy was dark and still. Its tall brick walls and jagged roof looked imposing and silent against the night sky. Nothing stirred.

He glanced down at his watch again. Allie was late. He was starting to get nervous.

They'd planned this night down to the tiniest detail but it was always a risky operation. The guards could have made their rounds at just the wrong moment and spotted her on the stairs. Or another student could have got up for a glass of water and seen Allie slipping down the hallway.

That was all it would take.

He wouldn't let himself think about any of the much worse possibilities. About Gabe or Nathaniel.

His jaw tightened and he squinted into the darkness. *If anything happens to her...*

His feelings towards Allie were intense – dangerously so. He'd never felt so strongly about anyone in his life. And no one knew better than him that this didn't make sense. Being in love with someone else's girlfriend was stupid. And he didn't do stupid things.

But this time – this *one time* – he couldn't seem to stop himself. There was something that drew him to her. He'd never met anyone so fragile and so strong at the same time. He hadn't known it was possible for those two attributes to exist in one person.

She fascinated him. And she could have been his…

…if I hadn't been such a bastard.

At his sides, Sylvain's hands clenched into fists. Every muscle in his body tightened with self-loathing.

Merde. Why am I thinking about this now?

Closing his eyes tight, he tried to shove the memories away.

Through sheer strength of will he made himself unclench his fists. He shook himself hard, loosening his muscles.

He would do anything to make it up to her. To win her trust again. To prove he'd changed. And that was why he was here now. Breaking all the Rules he'd sworn to uphold for a girl he could never have. Because she'd asked him to do it.

Leaning forwards, he looked up at the school again.

His breath caught. In the blue wash of moonlight, something moved.

He pulled a small set of binoculars out of his pocket and held them up to his eyes.

There.

Bent low and moving fast, Allie was running across the lawn, her footsteps so swift and smooth, from a distance she appeared to fly.

Under his breath, Sylvain cursed. He'd been so lost in his own thoughts he hadn't seen her leave the building.

Quickly, he scanned the grounds around her for any sign of pursuit but found nothing. She was safe for now. He turned the binoculars back towards her and watched as she swooped into the woods like a night bird.

The second she reached the secure cover of the tree line, he pocketed the binoculars and headed after her.

His eyes were fully adjusted to the dark by now and his steps were silent and sure. With the ease of practice, he avoided twigs and loose stones, anything that would make noise. He moved through the woods without a sound.

All his senses were alert. He was conscious of every rustle and creak in the forest as he searched for any sign that Allie was being followed by anyone except him.

He was good at tracking; very good at self-defence. But Gabe was out there somewhere tonight. And he was better.

Allie was quiet and careful but he still found her easily, even in the dark. She didn't have as much training as he did. He heard a faint splash as she stepped into water. The snap of a twig breaking into under her foot.

Ducking low behind a wild holly bush he watched her make her way down the footpath towards the stream. Again he scanned the area around her. Nothing. Despite the ruckus she was making, no one was following her.

In the distance, Allie clambered over a fallen tree, crashing noisily through the branches. Sylvain winced.

Well, if Gabe didn't know she was here before he knows it now.

After that Sylvain didn't try to hide from anyone who might be watching. If Gabe and Nathaniel were tracking Allie, they needed to know she wasn't alone.

The sound of roaring water let him know they were near the stream where the meeting would take place and he hurried ahead of her to the hiding spot he'd chosen earlier that day.

From there he watched Allie make her way tentatively down to the waterside. The recent rains had swollen the stream until its waters roiled. The moon turned the froth to sparkling silver.

She looked so alone standing there in the dark, hands flicking anxiously at her sides, Sylvain's heart went out to her. He knew how much this meant to her.

A sudden movement disturbed the trees across the stream and Allie looked up. Sylvain ducked lower as a young man stepped out onto the muddy stream bed. It was hard to see his face from this angle but he could hear his voice.

"Allie." The way he said her name was both familiar and tentative.

Even from a distance Sylvain could see her body tense.

"Christopher," she said, sounding as if she couldn't believe it was true.

So, this was the brother who'd ruined her life.

Tilting his head to one side, Sylvain studied him with open suspicion. He'd been curious about him ever since Jo had told him the story of how Allie ended up at Cimmeria. How her brother had run away, leaving a vicious note behind. The way the family had imploded. How Allie had struggled to bring her parents back to her by getting into trouble over and over again.

How instead that had just pushed everyone away.

And now, here she was, again. Putting her life in danger. Still trying to get her family back.

All because of her brother.

In the distance, Christopher took another step forwards and the moonlight caught his face. He had her grey eyes – otherwise there was little similarity in their appearance. He was tall and slim, with a tight, nervous stance. He kept glancing over his shoulder as if someone might creep up behind him.

At first, they talked about family things and how they'd missed each other. Christopher called her 'Allie-cat' and Sylvain could see how that touched her. It must be his pet name for her.

Then their conversation moved on to Lucinda and Christopher's expression changed. He looked angry now. Threatening.

Sylvain watched him closely for any sign that he might hurt her. But his anger seemed directed elsewhere.

"So, you know she lied to us our whole lives," Christopher was saying. "And that she and Isabelle conspired to keep us in the dark about our own family. And now our grandmother... " – he spat the word out with contempt – "...is denying us our family heritage. You do know that. Right?"

Allie held up her hands in a placating gesture. "Wait, wait, wait..." Her tone was soothing but steady. She didn't look frightened anymore. Now, she looked watchful. She was talking to him like an equal now, rather than a little sister. "How is Lucinda denying us anything?"

Good girl, Sylvain thought. *Don't let him confuse your emotions.*

"She refuses to acknowledge us as her family, Allie," Christopher said. He looked exasperated. "How can you not know this? It's all because of Isabelle. She's wheedled herself into Lucinda's good graces, replacing our mother. The last thing Isabelle wants now is for two kids to come along – real blood relatives – and take their rightful place as Lucinda's heirs. So, she's keeping you at Cimmeria where she can control you completely."

Sylvain's eyes narrowed. What he was saying was ridiculous. But the more Christopher talked, the more passionate he became. Now Allie was just trying to calm him down and to get him to say something more useful. Her goal was to find out what Nathaniel's plans were.

"You don't know her, Chris," Allie said. "She's not like that. She really cares about me . . . about our family."

"Oh, she does, does she?" The heat that had fired his previous words was gone, replaced by ice. "Then ask yourself this. Why did she lie about Ruth's death? And if you died, what would she say about you?"

What? Sylvain stared at Christopher in disbelief. *Is he trying to convince Allie that Isabelle is as bad as Nathaniel because of what happened with Ruth?*

It was ridiculous. *Gabe* killed Ruth. After that, Isabelle had no choice. The incident had to be hidden. With Nathaniel manipulating the police, any scandal could bring Isabelle down, and perhaps ruin the entire school.

Surely Allie understood this?

But in the moonlight, he saw Allie's shoulders slump. Christopher's words had done their job. He'd made her doubt the only adult she still trusted.

It was a cruel and heartless thing to do to her. And Sylvain could have happily punched her brother in the face for it, but this scene had to play out. So, he stayed still and let them talk. Christopher was raving about Nathaniel now.

"He's going to change everything. Fix all the things that have gone wrong in the world because the wrong people are in charge. Put the right people in charge. You know what Cimmeria is, right? I mean, what it's part of? If he ran the organisation, he could really do it, Allie. He could change everything. *Fix* everything."

Putain. Sylvain thought, disgusted. *He's an idiot. He sided with a dictator and now he needs her to join him so he doesn't have to realise he's made a horrible mistake.*

Allie asked all the right questions, trying to draw out more information. Christopher became charming again, talking about games they'd played as children, the trouble they'd got into.

At last, though, someone came for him. Sylvain could just see the figure of a man through the trees but couldn't make out his features. He said something quietly to Christopher, who turned back to Allie and said an abrupt goodbye.

Then, as quickly as they'd arrived, the two men slipped away into the night.

When they'd gone, Allie stood very still.

Her hands twisted together in front of her as she stared down into the rushing water of the stream.

Sylvain had to restrain himself from rushing down to her. She had to do this on her own. Silently he willed her to get it together – to follow the plan.

As if she'd heard his thoughts, she straightened and struck the tears from her cheeks with a quick swipe of her hand. Then with slow, determined steps she turned away from the water and followed the rocky path up to the chapel, as they'd agreed.

Shadowing her from some distance away, Sylvain allowed himself to feel relieved. They'd done it. The plan had gone off without a hitch. All they had to do now was get back to the school building. Then they could discuss everything they'd learned. And decide what to do next.

He was thinking about what he'd say, and how best to handle it, when Allie disappeared. One minute she was there on the path, and the next second she was gone. A frown creasing his brow, Sylvain stared at the spot where she should be. *Did she fall?* He stood still, holding his breath, waiting for her to reappear. Then he heard a muffled grunt, as if someone were lifting something heavy. His heart stuttered and he grasped the branch of the tree next to him.

Gabe stepped into the moonlight. In his arms, he held Allie in a vice-like grip.

She wasn't moving.

Everything switched to slow motion.

Sylvain had no chance to do anything but react. Gabe was moving fast and he wasn't trying to be quiet. Sylvain rushed through the woods, shadowing him as he'd earlier shadowed Allie. Only now his heart was filled with hate.

Hate filled him with cold clarity. Hate enhanced his senses and helped him move with stealth and speed. Hate gave him purpose.

Gabe had killed Ruth and betrayed them all. He was vicious. Sylvain had to get Allie away from him.

He kept his eyes on her body as he ran, willing her to move. She was so still, limp as toy in Gabe's grasp.

After a long, painful minute, she finally stirred. The rush of relief made Sylvain's knees weak.

She was OK.

At first she moved slowly, then she struggled in Gabe's arms, frantic to get away. But her movements were inefficient. Sylvain could see she was panicking.

Come on, Allie, he urged her silently. *Remember your training.*

He was close to them now. If Gabe had looked to his left he'd have seen him, matching him step for step. But Gabe's eyes remained straight ahead, as he walked with relentless purpose.

There must be a car waiting just off the grounds, Sylvain realised. They were taking Allie away – to Nathaniel.

She'd quit fighting now. Sylvain hoped that meant she'd come up with a plan.

Without warning, she swung her legs out and back, bending her knees so her feet kicked Gabe hard in the groin.

Even Gabe – with all his training and power – couldn't stand up to that kind of blow.

Crying out in pain, he doubled over, losing his grip on Allie, who tumbled hard to the ground.

She recovered from the fall quickly and scrabbled away, crawling on the ground but Gabe, still gasping for air, wasn't done yet. Quick as a snake, his hand shot out, grabbing her ankle and pulling her back.

Screaming in frustration and pain, Allie kicked hard at his hand but Gabe's grip was strong.

Sylvain was running at full speed now. Spotting a heavy, club-like branch on the side of the path, he grabbed it without breaking stride and hurtled towards them. Using all of his speed and power, he hit Gabe hard on the back of his head.

The cracking sound the wood made against Gabe's skull echoed in the quiet like a gunshot. The larger boy groaned and reached for the back of his head, releasing Allie.

But he didn't, as Sylvain had hoped, fall down.

Instead, he jumped to his feet and swung around to face him. His eyes were predatory, assessing and utterly without empathy.

"Sylvain, you bastard," he said. "That hurt."

Still holding the club, Sylvain kept his face fearless.

"Good," he said. "That was my intention."

Blood poured down one side of Gabe's face. His dark blonde hair was sticky with it. In the moonlight it looked black as tar.

Sylvain knew he needed to distract Gabe's attention away from Allie – give her a chance to get away. He circled the taller boy like a panther, bouncing lightly on his heels as if he wanted nothing more right now than a fight with a psychopath.

"Well." Gabe gave a lazy grin. "Let's do this."

In a movement Sylvain would spend months trying to figure out, Gabe duck and spun so quickly his body was a blur. Caught off guard, Sylvain swung at him but Gabe had angled himself perfectly. Grabbing the club with ruthless strength, he twisted it in under-and-over manoeuvre.

If Sylvain hadn't let go it would have broken his wrist.

Now it was Gabe's club.

Looking up, Sylvain saw Allie standing at the edge of the path, eyes wide.

"Run, Allie." He kept his voice steady and calm, hoping this would convince her that he was in control.

He should have known better.

She shook her head stubbornly. "I'm not leaving you."

Some part of him was touched by this – given hope. But if she stayed this was all for nothing.

Her misguided sense of loyalty would get them both killed.

"Run," he said again, raising his voice. "*Now*."

Gabe, who had his back to her so he could keep his eyes on Sylvain, spoke up then. "Yes. Run, Allie. You don't want to see this. I'll come get you in a minute. And I will pay you back for kicking me in the balls."

His words sent a chill down Sylvain's spine but he kept his gaze on Allie, begging her with his eyes to heed his request. Because of that, he almost missed it when Gabe swung the makeshift club at his head.

The only warning Sylvain had was the look of horror on Allie's face. Moving on instinct, he ducked to the right but the club struck him a glancing blow that forced a cry of pain from him.

He couldn't argue with Allie any more. He had to be in this thing completely.

No one had ever beat Gabe in training. He was the best fighter Night School had ever produced. And this fight was real.

Recovering, Sylvain whirled and lowered his centre of gravity to hit Gabe hard with an elbow in the torso. It was like punching a rock. Pain shot down his arm.

He heard the air leave Gabe's lungs, but the other boy didn't look like it hurt him as much as it had hurt Sylvain.

He glanced back to where Allie had stood but she was gone.

He hoped she was running fast. If she could bring back help they might stand a chance.

But even as he thought it he knew it was hopeless. There wasn't time. They were nearly a mile from the school building. By the time help arrived he'd be dead.

Still, at least Allie would be safe.

And that was what mattered.

He'd taken things from her when they first met – her faith in people. Her trust.

At least he could give her the chance to live.

Watching his expression, Gabe's lips turned up in a sardonic grin. "She's gone now. You can relax. Bloody hell, Sylvain, I can't believe you're messing with Carter's girl. That's not like you. Usually you like them all fresh and unsullied."

His words struck a nerve and Sylvain spun a whirling kick at his face, but Gabe ducked the blow, swiping his foot away like a cat toying with a mouse, and punched Sylvain hard in the temple. The blow sent him reeling.

His head *rang*. Warm blood gushed down the side of his face making it hard to see.

I must have a cut above my eye, he thought, trying to stay rational. *It's nothing*.

"You'll have to try harder than that, Sylvain," Gabe taunted him. "Have you been too busy messing with Carter's sloppy seconds to practice? Looks like she's got you whipped."

Sylvain's fist caught him on the jaw this time, a square blow that made Gabe's neck twist.

"You'll pay for that." Gabe whirled on him with a roar.

Moving fast, Sylvain dodged him, aiming a kick at his knee as he passed. But Gabe was faster. Catching Sylvain's foot he flipped him high into the air.

For a second, the world spun. Then Sylvain landed with such force all the air left his lungs. Some part of him wanted nothing so much as to lie there. But he couldn't. Allie needed time to get back to the school building. He had to keep Gabe here longer.

With a groan, he staggered to his feet. But as he weaved his way back to the path it occurred to him that he would lose this fight. And that Gabe wouldn't stop until he killed him.

"Come on, Sylvain." Gabe said, cracking his knuckles."Don't give up now. I'm just starting to have fun."

Sylvan spit blood on the ground. Then he turned to face his enemy again, hands clenched in front of him.

"Why are you here?" he heard himself ask.

"What is that? A philosophical question?" Gabe's expression turned icy. "I'm here because my boss sent me. I'm here to collect a package and go home. That's all I wanted to do but you got in the way."

The punches seemed to come faster this time. Sylvain's reactions were getting slower. But he held his own until Gabe's fist struck him square in the jaw. For a split second, everything went dark, then it zoomed horribly back into focus again.

Shaking his head to clear it, he again pried himself up off the cold earth.

It was hard to see through the blood and sweat. Gabe looked blurry and indistinct. The night took on a kind of hazy unreality. Like he was watching himself fight and fall from far away.

Every part of his body hurt but he thought he could still kick. He struggled forwards for one last try. Gabe smiled.

Grabbing Sylvain's left arm, Gabe twisted it behind him sending a sharp pain through his shoulder. Sylvain struggled to free himself but each movement made the pain worse. He heard himself cry out.

Then Gabe wrapped his other arm tightly across his neck.

Sylvain was trapped.

"That was an amateur's mistake, Sylvain," Gabe tutted. "I'm disappointed. You used to be so good. What would Raj Patel say?"

He tightened his arm across Sylvain's throat, cutting off his air.

Tendrils of panic wrapped around Sylvain's chest. He knew self-defence; he understood the concepts of hand-to-hand combat. So, he knew this game was over. There was no way to free himself from this.

His hands gripped Gabe's arm, but he had no strength. Without oxygen he'd be unconscious in seconds. He could hear himself wheezing.

"Oh, Sylvain," Gabe said pityingly. "What a way to go. All alone in the woods, beaten by the traitor. All because of Carter's girl. Who would have believed it?"

Sylvain wanted to fight but he couldn't seem to move. His hands dropped to his sides. His eyes fluttered shut.

Gabe was wrong. It wasn't a bad way to go, really.

Suddenly, he heard a shriek. Gabe's entire body shuddered. His arms loosened and Sylvain fell free.

He couldn't remember hitting the ground. The next thing he knew, Allie was there, fear in her eyes, pulling him to his feet with all her strength.

I must be dreaming.

"Allie?" He tried to say the word, but his mouth wouldn't seem to work. His whole face felt broken.

Her arm was tight around his waist and he wanted to tell her it was hurting his ribs but he couldn't say that either.

He looked around for Gabe and saw him lying on the path, a broken stake sticking out of his shoulder.

"You little bitch," Gabe gasped, glaring at Allie. "You stabbed me." Grasping the stake, he tried to pull it out then screamed again, letting go.

The fear disappeared from Allie's eyes. Replaced by rage.

"You little . . ."

"Yeah I know, 'bitch'," she snapped, cutting him off. "You said that already."

Adrenaline was making her brave and she leaned towards Gabe to say something else but Sylvain found the strength to hold onto her and pull her back to him.

Surprised, she turned to look at him.

"We have to run," Sylvain explained reasonably, but the words came out as garbled mush.

"What is it?" she asked, leaning closer to him.

She looked so brave.

He took a deep breath. He ordered himself not to feel the pain. And he pulled her with him as he took a step. And then another.

"We have to *run*," he said again, more clearly this time.

This time he knew she understood, because she turned with him, and they ran together into the darkness.

A Very Early Prequel

When I was promoting *Night School Fracture*, a press agent had the idea of getting a short story set in the Night School world in a British magazine. It seemed like a good idea. To be honest, I was thrilled to find out there were still magazines publishing short stories at all. I would never have thought to say no, or to ask too many questions. Then, though, I spent ages thinking up a story to write. It couldn't be "just" young adult, the magazine editors insisted. "No adults want to read about teenagers." (LOL. *Twilight* and *Hunger Games* and *Harry Potter,* but sure, editor. You believe that.) So I decided to write a story from Isabelle's perspective. I'd always wanted to get into her mind, and this was my chance.

You guys, I worked on this for *days*. It wasn't easy to write. Like Allie, I had always seen Isabelle as a loving but distant authority figure. Now I had to truly understand her. To see the nuts and bolts of her. In the end, I think it took me more than a week to find the story, to find her, to understand her relationship with Raj all those years ago, to envision the school back then. And to do the math and figure out how old Carter would have been.

And then the bloody magazine *turned the story down*.

They said it wasn't "adult" enough, which made me *RAGE*. It was so infuriating. But it's also typical of the snobbery in publishing and media around young adult fiction. I am forever saying, "*Salinger* wrote young adult fiction, you absolute cretins. *Romeo and Juliet* is young adult fiction, you knuckle-dragging imbeciles." And I don't know, but maybe that's why they don't like me?

Anyway, I truly hope that so-called editor has seen the error of her ways. Or maybe she's still publishing moving stories about women in love their washing machines.

This story is set six years before Night School begins. Carter is 10 years old. Isabelle is thirty. And everything is about to go terribly wrong.

Anger flickered like

flames in his dark, brown

eyes. They'd known each

other since they were

teenagers.

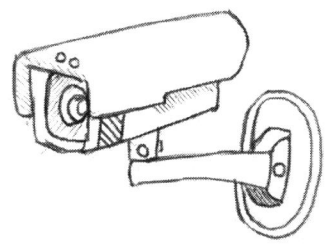

The Day the Lights Went Out

- ISABELLE -

"What's wrong with it? It looks fine to me."

Isabelle le Fanult stared at the computer screen, bending over to see the monitor. Colours flashed, and the school's logo came up just as it should.

"Look closely." Raj Patel clicked the mouse again. "There." He pointed at the screen. "Did you see that?"

One web page segued smoothly to the next. Isabelle could see nothing wrong. Exasperated, she held up her hands.

"It hitches," Raj explained, demonstrating again. "Right there. There's a slight hesitation when you click on any link. As if it's going through a process it shouldn't go through."

Cocking her head to one side, Isabelle held his gaze. "OK. So, it hitches. Why are you telling me this?"

The girl sitting at the computer next to Raj leaned over towards them. The light sparkled off her narrow glasses and made her dark skin gleam.

"Because," she said in an American accent, "it shouldn't hitch. And every computer in the school is doing precisely the same thing. It started last night and we can't trace the reason why."

The girl's voice was flat and steady. She didn't openly betray any excitement, but Isabelle could see the nervousness in the way she held her hands, curled into tight fists.

Isabelle shot Raj a look and he shrugged.

"Dom discovered it first," he said, with a hint of embarrassment. "She's been working on this all day."

"You'd have noticed it eventually." Dom spoke without taking her gaze from the monitor.

She looked younger than her fifteen years – her figure was slim, and her black hair was clipped short and boyish – but Isabelle knew better than to dismiss her concerns.

Raj was in charge of security, but Dom had helped him with tech for more than a year now. Everyone in the school found her both impressive and a little scary. When it came to computers, there was almost nothing she couldn't do.

***

The headmistress ran a hand wearily through her hair. It was late in the afternoon and her unruly locks had begun to escape from the clips that held them in place.

"The computers are networked," she said doubtfully. "Aren't they supposed to act the same?"

Dom rolled her eyes but said nothing. Isabelle got the feeling she was restraining herself.

Raj kept his tone patient. "They're not supposed to act at all, Izzy. They're supposed to work normally and they almost are. But something's changed in the last twenty-four hours. I think we've been hacked. By someone who is very, very good at it."

"I just," Dom muttered, "can't find the hack code."

Isabelle turned her sharp eyes to the computer again. It sat in front of her, humming normally, a web page flooding its screen with primary colours.

"But you haven't been able to find any evidence of the hack other than this?"

Raj shook his head. "Whoever's done it is skilled. We're still trying to figure out what they're after."

For the first time since this conversation began, a nervous chill ran down Isabelle's spine.

Cimmeria was home to children of the country's elite families. These were the offspring of billionaires, prime ministers and princes. They needed to be kept safe. All of them were vulnerable to kidnap and extortion. Each of them was worth a fortune to the wrong kinds of people.

Raj was one of the best security chiefs in the country – in addition to protecting Cimmeria, he ran a private security firm that included the prime minister among its clients. On his recommendation they'd already increased their CCTV, enhanced the electronic fences and replaced the school's locks with state of the art equipment.

Cimmeria may have looked like a school but in reality it was a fortress.

They were safe here. Isabelle was certain of it.

Straightening the hem of her black cashmere cardigan, she turned towards the door of the computer room, signalling the end of their discussion.

"Thank you for letting me know. Come back to me when you have something more concrete, Raj."

But his voice followed her out into the hallway.

"I don't like it, Izzy," he called after her. "This could be bad."

The headmistress didn't look back. Having spent a small fortune on the other security enhancements, she wasn't about to replace all the school's computers just because Raj was nervous. Besides, it was probably just kids anyway. All kids were good at computers these days. Look at Dom.

Still, Raj's concern was sobering, and as she walked from the classroom wing into the main building, Isabelle barely noticed the marble statues arrayed around her. The school's oak-panelled walls had been polished until they gleamed. Above her head crystal chandeliers sparkled like diamonds.

She'd been headmistress for nearly a year now. Raj had been with her the whole time.

This was the first time she could remember seeing him nervous.

She replayed Dom's words in her mind, trying to decide how concerned she should be.

The truth was, they were all a little paranoid right now. It was that damned letter that had done it.

It had been a statement of intent, without question. "What you have should be mine . . . If you don't return my inheritance to me I will take it back, Isabelle. One brick at a time if necessary . . . You know I can do it,,,"

Her lips tightened at the memory of those words, written in her step-brother's familiar, slanted script.

Nathaniel had taken the news of her promotion to headmistress very badly. He'd threatened Lucinda, insulted the Board. He was vengeful and unstable – they had to be careful. But surely that was all hot air. He'd get it out of his system and move on. He'd never done anything violent before.

And yet...

The tone of that letter was different. It had been ice cold. And he'd stolen Lucinda's papers and disappeared.

What if he had been planning this all along? What if this was just the start?

Isabelle shook her head as if to make the thought go away. A slight time lag in computer responsiveness seemed like a minor problem. The IT guys could sort it out. Or Dom would fix it.

They simply couldn't afford to panic every time something seemed slightly off-kilter.

"Coming through!" A dark-haired boy tore past her, his navy blue school jumper rucked up from the speed of his movements.

"Carter. A moment, please." Isabelle didn't raise her voice but her air of authority was unmistakeable.

Skidding to a stop, the boy turned back. Huge brown eyes gazed up at her from beneath a lowered brow. A shock of dark hair tumbled forwards to his eyebrows. He had a graze on his nose and she wondered if he'd been in another fight. He'd never tell her, even if she asked.

A wave of protectiveness washed over her and she struggled to resist the urge to hug him. She cared about him so much he might as well be her own child. She'd helped to raise him after his parents died seven years ago. But he was nearly twelve years old now, and he needed to realise the school's rules applied to him, too.

"No running in the halls. You know the rules." She glanced at her watch. "What are you doing out here? Shouldn't you be in maths?"

Carter blinked at her guilelessly. "That's why I was running. I'm late. Bankston's going to kill me."

Despite herself, Isabelle's lips quirked up. It was impossible to discipline a child with eyes like that.

"Make your way directly to class at a reasonable speed," she said, feigning sternness. "Tell Mr Bankston you have my permission to be late this one time."

Without another word, he whirled and hurtled away.

The headmistress raised her voice, "But don't do it again. And I said reasonable speed."

At the end of the hall, Carter skipped as he tried to force himself to slow down.

She fought back another smile. He'd had a growth spurt recently – suddenly he was nearly as tall as her. The girls were starting to notice him. Things would change for Carter soon – she hoped he was ready for it. After all he'd been through…

The phone in her pocket buzzed and she answered it brusquely. "Isabelle."

It was one of the security guards. "Something's wrong. The gate keeps opening and closing on its own. We can't seem to control it."

"Oh, good." Isabelle pinched the bridge of her nose between her thumb and forefinger. Her day just kept getting worse. "The computers are acting up, too. Let's get Raj's IT guys to look at this – maybe there's a wiring problem."

"I'll call him," the guard said doubtfully. "But it doesn't look like a wiring problem to me."

Isabelle stopped walking. "What do you mean?"

"I don't know, exactly," the guard said. "It's just … it's not randomly opening and closing. It's moving with intelligence. If you reach for it, it pulls away. You turn your back and it slams open. It's as if it can see us." He paused as if deciding to say what he said next. "I think someone's operating it from outside the school."

Isabelle's heart stuttered. "How could they do that?" she asked. "t's a gate."

"Yeah, it's a gate. But it's an electric gate wired into the school's mainframe computer."

An awful feeling of inevitability chilled Isabelle's blood. If someone hacked the computers could they hack the CCTV?

"I don't like it . . ." Raj had said.

She turned back towards the computer lab and broke into a run. "Call Raj on his mobile," she said, her voice urgent and breathless. "Tell him what's happening. Tell him I'm on my way to him now."

In the wide, empty hallway her panicked footsteps echoed incongruously. Around her, oil paintings of regal women in silk and pearls, and bearded men in stiff, 19th-century suits, stared down at her with disapproval as she rushed back towards the classroom wing.

What are you doing to our school? their faces seemed to say. *We trusted you. You must protect it.*

As she ran, questions circulated in Isabelle's mind. Would Nathaniel really do this? Would he go this far? Would he attack Cimmeria Academy?

She didn't want to answer that last question. She didn't even want to think about it. She wanted to get back to Raj and work this thing out. Fast.

She was almost there when the lights went out.

From the classrooms around her Isabelle heard gasps as the overhead projectors and computers powered down. It was a bright, sunny day – she could still easily see where she was going, but she slowed down anyway – her ribs seemed to compress her lungs and her breath came in short gasps.

The gates, the computers, the lights. This was no coincidence.

"Everyone stay in your seats . . ." The commanding voices of teachers filtering through the closed doors helped her to focus.

A nearby door opened and Jerry Cole peered out at her, blinking owlishly through his glasses. "Isabelle? What's going on?"

She forced herself to sound normal and in control as she spoke to the science teacher. "Keep the children in the classroom. Let the other teachers know to do the same. I'm going to see Raj – find out what's happening."

She saw concern dawn in his face.

"Raj...?"

She didn't stop to explain why she was seeing the security consultant about a power outage. There wasn't time.

In the now-dim computer room, and surrounded by dead screens, Raj was on his phone, issuing a steady flow of commands. Next to him, Dom was feverishly typing on her laptop. Powered by battery, it was the only computer still working.

"Trace it through the external sites . . ." Raj was saying. "Yes, I know how they work but you know how we work. Get it done. See if you can find who's behind this."

He set down his phone and looked at her – she asked the question with her eyes.

"It's a deliberate attack," he said quietly. Isabelle lowered her head to her hands as he continued. "The computers, the phone system, the gate, the lights – anything connected to the school's server is compromised."

"Can we get the lights back on at least?" She looked through the window. It would be dark in four hours. The building housed more than two hundred students – they couldn't sit in the dark.

"We're trying," he said.

Isabelle's phone buzzed.

"Isabelle," she snapped.

"Explain this email, Isabelle. Has something happened?" Lucinda's tone was crisp.

She was chair of the Board that ran the school; Isabelle wanted nothing more than to hang up on her, but you don't hang up on the boss. Particularly this one.

"What email?" Isabelle couldn't keep the impatience out of her voice. "I'm very busy right—"

89

"I'll read it to you," Lucinda said. " 'With immediate effect, I hereby tender my resignation as headmistress of Cimmeria Academy and any and all roles I hold within...' "

The room began to spin. Isabelle gripped the back of the chair in front of her. "I don't... "

Something in her voice alerted Raj; he looked up at her sharply.

"It was sent to everyone on the Board from your email address." Lucinda said. "Please tell me what it means."

"I didn't send that email, Lucinda." Isabelle felt sick. "The school is being attacked. It's Nathaniel."

The pause that followed was significant. When Lucinda spoke again her tone was guarded. "How?"

"What email, Izzy?" Raj leaned forwards to meet her gaze.

Looking at him, Isabelle realised only he and Dom could get them out of this mess. Suddenly, she knew what she needed to do.

"Lucinda, reply to everyone who received that email. Tell them we've been hacked. Tell them we're investigating the source now. I'll call you back soon. We might need your help."

Ending the call, she turned to Raj. "Nathaniel has issued my resignation from all my positions on the board and at the school."

Anger flickered like flames in his dark, brown eyes. They'd known each other since they were teenagers. In some ways, he'd always been her protector.

"So, he's hacked our email," he said. "And our server – that's what the hitch was. Everything's being routed through a number of servers around the world that hide the user's location. We're tracing it now but . . ."

"... it'll take a little time," Dom said, finishing his thought.

In Isabelle's pocket, her phone buzzed again.

Like a wasp, she thought, *caught in a jar.*

"The lights, Raj," she said, pulling it out. "Get the lights on."

She accepted the call without looking at the phone. "I will call you back, Lucinda..."

"Hello, Isabelle. It's been a while."

Nathaniel's voice, once so familiar, stopped her in her tracks. Without thinking, she reached out for Raj – as if he could fight Nathaniel for her now, on the phone.

"Nathaniel, why are you doing this?"

She heard Dom's quick intake of breath.

Raj leapt to his feet, punching numbers into his phone, waiting impatiently for someone to answer. "He's on Isabelle's phone now." He spoke into the receiver quietly. "Find out where he is."

"You know why." Nathaniel, like Isabelle, retained only the faintest hint of a Scottish accent. They'd both lived in England too long. Sometimes Isabelle thought it was like their past had happened to other people.

"You stole from me." His voice was cold and distant. As if he was far, far away from her, in every way.

Isabelle pressed her fingertips against her forehead. "I know why you think you have to do this, Nathaniel. We can talk about it, the unfairness. But there are children here. Please. Just stop this."

"I will stop. As soon as you do what I've asked." His voice made her skin crawl. "Give me my inheritance. Give me Cimmeria and the Board. Give me our father's corporation. Give back what you stole."

"I didn't steal it." Isabelle heard the heat in her voice and paused, trying to even her tone. "It was given to me. You saw the will, Nathaniel. I stole nothing. Father chose me. Not you. And I don't know why—"

He didn't let her finish. "And you chose to keep it even though you knew it was wrong. It was mine by tradition. By heredity. By family law. Father is dead so I can't make him give it to me. But you, little sister … you are still here. So, I have come to you. Do what's right and I will make this stop. Refuse, and I will make you and Lucinda Meldrum suffer in ways you cannot imagine."

For a moment, Isabelle couldn't believe what she was hearing. She'd always known he was vindictive, but she hadn't realised he was capable of this.

She struggled to keep her voice reasonable.

"This is absurd, Nathaniel. You have to give up this bizarre obsession that the family robbed you. You were well taken care of."

He ignored her words as if she hadn't spoken.

"This can get worse." Nathaniel's voice was low and threatening. "Much, much worse. People could get hurt. You can stop it now, Isabelle."

"Every computer," Raj was saying into his phone as Dom typed faster and faster. "Every server and anything connected to it. Everything that can be hacked. Rip them all out."

"Nathaniel don't be ridiculous. We can work this out-" Isabelle began, but Nathaniel cut her off.

"This is just the beginning," he said.

Then he hung up.

For a long moment, Isabelle stood holding the silent receiver to her ear. Only when she finally dropped her hand did she realise she was trembling.

Through the doorway she could hear the sounds of excited conversation from the classrooms, and teachers trying to keep order. All the things you'd expect to hear when the lights went out. But her heart still pounded in her ears.

She turned to Raj but before she could speak a click and a buzz signalled the return of electricity. The room flooded with light.

Down the hallway, the students cheered.

But the computers didn't come back on – Raj had unplugged every one.

In the strange silence of the computer room, Isabelle turned to Raj, forcing herself to appear calm. "How did he do it?"

"Whoever is working for him is very good," Raj said with reluctant admiration. "From what we can tell so far, they've hacked into every device we've got. It appears they started with the mainframe, and that gave them access to the networked computers, through which they accessed CCTV, electronic gate, phones." His voice was calm but she could see the anger in his gaze. "Everything."

"How did he access the mainframe?" Isabelle asked.

Raj hesitated. "It had to be done in person."

Anger brought heat to Isabelle's face. "He was here? In my school?"

"Someone was here," Raj said. "Someone who worked for him."

Isabelle's world was crashing around her. She'd worked so hard to take control of this school. It was part of her. Now it felt invaded.

Tainted.

"How is that possible, Raj? We vet everyone."

"No system is perfect, Isabelle. And you know Nathaniel is very good. He's one of us. He knows how we work."

Someone tapped at the door. It swung open to reveal Jerry Cole's concerned face. "What's going on? Is everything OK?"

Raj and Isabelle exchanged a look. Cole was new but they both liked him. He was sharp and talented. Raj inclined his head.

Isabelle cleared her throat and tried to look confident and in control. "It's Nathaniel. The computers are compromised. We're working on it." Jerry's mouth formed an 'o' of surprise but before he could speak, Isabelle turned back to Raj. "Can we make them safe?"

He shook his head. "Anything electronic that looks out can be used to look in. Anything can be hacked."

There was no decision to make, really. They couldn't let Nathaniel do this again.

"They all have to go," she said.

Raj nodded but Jerry and Dom both stared at them both as if they'd gone mad. It was the first time Dom had stopped typing since the crisis began.

"No computers at all?" Jerry said, his voice ringing with disbelief. "In a school? Come on, Isabelle, that's not feasible. Parents won't stand for it. You can't…"

"My decision is final, Jerry." Isabelle fixed him with a hard stare. "We don't have any choice. Raj will look for a way to build a secure network but if it can't be done then…" She shrugged, as if it didn't matter that the school wouldn't have computers. "We have no alternative."

Dom looked as if she wanted to speak, but Raj rested a warning hand on her shoulder.

"The parents won't—" Jerry began.

Isabelle held up her hand. Her head was beginning to pound. She couldn't do this right now.

"Go see to your students, Jerry. We will discuss this later."

The science teacher left with obvious reluctance, closing the door behind him. When he'd gone, Raj turned back to Isabelle. "He's right, you know. Parents are going to see this as a failure."

Isabelle straightened her spine. "Then Lucinda and I will convince them it is an advantage. Their children will learn to study instead of spending time playing online. No distractions. Old-fashioned hard work. Anyway, selling this is our job. Your job is to find out what Nathaniel is planning and stop him."

Silence fell, heavy with unspoken words. It was Raj who broke it.

His expression held a warning. "Isabelle, he'll never give up. He's obsessed."

It was a terrifying thought – her own half-brother hated her so much he wanted nothing more in life than to destroy her.

They had been close once, a long time ago. But that, like childhood, was over. Now she had to start treating him like the stranger he had become.

Isabelle walked to the door. Only when she opened it did she reply, her voice cold as ice.

"Neither will I."

The Ultimate Prequel

In March 2020, the world ended. Not forever (I hope, anyway. I'm writing this in September 2020, and I'd like to think that you're reading this in 2021 and the world is still here), but for a while at least the pandemic shut down everything, including publishing. All my books were put on hold. The release of *Number 10* was pushed back in most territories and languages. The espionage novel I was writing could not be submitted to publishers because no publishers were at work. Everything. Just. Stopped.

As the weeks passed and we remained trapped in our houses with almost no grocery deliveries and toilet paper and coffee shortages, I started to feel that I needed to create something good out of all the chaos. My career was on hold. Our lives were on hold. But I still had words. So I went onto Instagram and proposed writing some Night School stories. I made a list of ideas of what I might write, and let everyone vote. This story won by a landslide. I'm not sure I've seen a clearer result in any election in the last decade.

I wrote this without an outline or much of an idea, and the story fell into place on its own. It's set in 1987, when Isabelle and Raj are students at Cimmeria. Isabelle is just as I expected her to be — practical, thoughtful, and a tiny bit mischievous. The real surprise for me was Raj. He's a proper ladies' man, breaking hearts and taking names. I've got to say, I did not see that coming. The other surprise was Allie's mum, who is a total wild child. And I love everything about her, from her big hair to her short skirts. She makes me happy.

I've only written two chapters of this story and I would love to write more. Hopefully I will one day, but first I have to finish the Number

10 series, and this adult book I'm writing, and my crime series. But if I can carve out the time, I promise I'll come back to this.

In the meantime, here's Night School 1987.

Why would he want
someone like her, when all
the glittering girls were his
for the taking?

Night School 1987
– PART 1 –

The last lesson of the day had barely ended but the students were already spilling into the wide school corridors, a moving sea of navy blue blazers, their voices rising with every step away from another day of learning until they formed a cacophony of relief.

Oblivious to the noise and the others' rush to get outside, Isabelle lingered in the doorway of her history classroom, flipping through her notebook, a small, worried frown crinkling her forehead.

Her teacher stopped next to her, briefcase in his hand. The sunlight pouring through the windows lit up his grey hair until it was the blinding white of snow. "What's the matter, Miss St. John? Did you lose something?"

She glanced up at him. "I'm sorry, Mr Hollis. I just want to make sure I got everything you said in the last five minutes. I was writing very quickly but I might have missed something."

His eyebrows rose, just a little. "I appreciate your dedication. If you have any questions you can run them by me on Monday."

"Oh, thank you!" Isabelle smiled at him, and put her notebook away.

"You know," the teacher said, "you've been doing much better these last few weeks." He tapped the side of his nose. "Don't think I haven't noticed."

Isabelle beamed at him. "Well, I've been working very hard. I feel like I'm getting somewhere."

"Keep it up." Turning away, he headed into the throng of students, raising his voice. "Quiet down, all of you. This isn't a gymnasium. You are not *performers*."

As soon as he was gone, she hurried in the opposite direction. As she passed the next classroom along, her arm was grabbed, and she was hustled towards the stairs.

"You still working on old Hollis?" Raj whispered the words into her ear, a wicked note beneath his thick, Yorkshire accent. "Trying to get him to forgive you for skivving off last week when you were supposed to be in his class?"

Isabelle blinked at him innocently. "I don't know what you're talking about. You know how dedicated I am to studying history."

Raj gave a low laugh and loosened his hold on her elbow. Isabelle wished he wouldn't let go.

"You're wasting your time," he said, slipping his blazer off and draping it over his arm as he began to loosen his blue-and-white tie. "I mean, it's not like you'll ever get in real trouble. You could get away with murder here."

Isabelle smiled as they followed the throng to the stairs. They both knew her teachers liked her – she worked hard and made good grades. They'd forgive the occasional infraction.

"How was physics?" she asked. "Didn't you have a mock exam today?"

"Oh, God. Don't remind me." He shuddered. "It was brutal. But I think I did OK." He stretched his arms above his head. He was stocky and athletic enough that she could see the shape of his muscles through the fabric of his shirt. "Man," he complained, "I am so tired of sitting in a classroom. I need to get outside. Run around."

It was hard to think when he did that muscle flexing thing. Isabelle scrambled for something to say. What came out was, of course, the wrong thing. "Did you know that, whenever you sit, you constantly exchange electrons with the chair?" He gave her a quizzical look but she kept going, unable to stop herself. "By the end of a 50-minute lesson, you have more of the chair's electrons than your own."

"So you're saying I'm a chair now?"

"Basically."

She could not imagine why, out of every fact she knew, her brain had offered her that one. Sometimes she thought her own brain hated her.

"Well," Raj said amiably, "that explains a lot."

As they walked on, she studied him from the corner of her eye. His glossy brown hair was thick and wavy above soulful, dark eyes. His eyelashes were *insane*. She would kill for lashes like that. His hands hung loose at his sides, as he studied the crowd around them with a curious intensity that she suspected missed nothing in the busy space. He would tell her later about what he'd observed – who was breaking up, and who was falling in love. Who was still angry about something that had happened earlier, and who was quietly depressed and in need of attention. It was this extraordinary awareness that had first attracted her to him when he'd arrived at the school two years ago on a scholarship. In the otherwise exclusively white school, his darker skin made him stand out. It was the first thing she'd noticed when she saw him walking up the stairs with his suitcase. The second was the way he held his head high, his eyes always meeting those of anyone who passed him. Never flinching.

Bravery was the characteristic she admired most. And she could tell from the start that he had it. In spades.

The only problem was, he didn't seem to see her as anything other than a friend. She'd given him every chance to notice she was actually a girl, but he never seemed to see it. Half the girls in their year group were in love with him. He never wanted for attention, and maybe that was why he didn't notice her waiting, hoping he'd choose her.

She tried not to let it hurt her, but…

The two of them walked side-by-side, their steps in easy sync as they navigated the twisting halls of Cimmeria Academy's classroom wing, following the others through the double doors into the central atrium, where statues clustered and their voices echoed off the hard floor and high ceiling.

It was a grand old building, but it had grown dingy. The paintings on the walls were dusty, the ornate, gilt frames dulled by dirt and time. The chandeliers had broken or missing facets, and the afternoon light caught the strands of cobwebs draped between them and made them glisten like silk.

In some sections it was worse than others. The dining hall was the worst, she thought. At some point they'd lowered the ceilings to make the big room easier to heat, so the acoustic tiles cut off the top of the huge fireplace, making it look broken. All the rooms were like that – the heat didn't work in the dorm rooms. The ballroom floor was scratched and dull, its huge windows so overgrown with vines that they no longer let in a hint of light. And the library was in a state. Books were damaged and stacked everywhere. The keys to the study carrels had been lost, so they could no longer be used. Half the lights in there were out – it was so dark, the students frequently joked that you had to check out a book just so you could take it into the hallway and see what the title was. It all contributed to a sense of mismanagement and neglect.

"I wish they'd fix this place up," she muttered, kicking a piece of litter out of the way. "They barely even clean it anymore."

Raj glanced around at the statues decorating the atrium, the marble grey with dust. "Big buildings like this are expensive to maintain," he said. "Taxes are probably huge on this place. Must cost them a fortune just to heat it."

Isabelle shrugged that off. "They should just ask our parents for money if they need it. Everyone who goes here has parents who could afford to pitch in."

"Not everyone." His tone was gentle but meaningful, and she flushed.

"Of course. Not everyone." She put her hand on his arm in silent apology. His easy smile told her none was needed. Still, she felt like an idiot. Raj's father was in the Army, serving in Northern Ireland. He didn't make much money.

"*Your* dad should bloody pony up, though," he said, when an awkward silence fell. "Get this place dusted, if nothing else."

"I blame Fergie," she told him. "He's running this place down."

"Maybe your dad could have him dusted, too," Raj suggested.

George Ferguson had been headmaster at Cimmeria for about forty years. Now in his seventies, he was so rarely seen at the school rumours abounded that he'd secretly retired and no one on the board had noticed.

"I keep telling my dad he should do something. But he's too busy to notice stuff like this. He says the school always needs work." She sighed, as they moved into the school's main hallway, panelled in oak that badly needed a polish. "I should tell Lucinda. She's the one who really gets things done."

Raj frowned, lost for a second. "Oh wait. That's Lucinda Meldrum, right? Your dad's ex?" She'd explained all this before, but when she gave an impatient nod, he pointed out, "Your family is more confusing than my physics homework."

She couldn't really argue. "It's my dad's fault. He keeps getting married. There are so many women in his life even I lose track. Anyway, since he and my mum got divorced, I hardly ever see him. I'm not convinced he always remembers who I am." She stopped outside the common room and leaned back against the wall, watching the other students move by. "I'm terrified that one day he'll get me confused with one of his wives."

Raj gave a scandalised laugh but Isabelle was already distracted.

"Speaking of Lucinda – look, there's Elizabeth." She pointed to a slim girl with dark hair teased up into a storm of waves. She was at the centre of a group of other girls, all of them just as heavily made up, but none stood out like her. Her smile lit up her face, creating perfectly symmetrical dimples in her full cheeks. The others were all watching her with open admiration.

"Lizzie! Over here!" Isabelle raised her arm and waved. As she watched, the girl said something that made the others laugh, and then bounced over to them, her skirt swishing with every step.

"Hey, Iz." She turned the full, 100-watt glow of her attention on Raj, studying him with a cheeky tilt of her head. "I swear to almighty God, Raj, you get cuter every single day."

He grinned down at her. "Right back at you."

They looked cute together – Elizabeth small and adorable, and Raj all muscles and perfect hair.

Isabelle hated that she was so jealous. But nobody could resist Elizabeth when she wanted to be noticed. She always turned up the waistband of her skirt to raise the hem and better show off her legs. She'd already been written up three times this term for loosening her tie and unbuttoning the top three buttons of her blouse to reveal the smooth skin beneath. With her make-up carefully applied, and her hair fluffed until she looked exactly like the singers they watched on Top of the Pops and MTV, she never failed to attract attention.

A few feet away from where they were standing, a mottled antique mirror hung above an ornate marble table and, as the two of them flirted, she glanced at herself condemningly. It seemed to her that she looked drab by comparison to Liz. Too tall, too pale, too thin. Her long hair had a good golden-brown hue, but she couldn't control its curls, so she wore it pulled back in a pony tail most days, and still it kept escaping, frizzing around her face. Everything about her was wrong.

For the first time, she felt hopeless. No wonder Raj only saw her as a friend. Why would he want someone like her, when all the glittering girls were his for the taking?

"What were you two talking about anyway?" Elizabeth asked, bringing her into the conversation.

It took Isabelle a second to remember. "Oh, I was just trying to explain to Raj how I'm sort of not related to your mum."

Elizabeth winced. "Oh, don't. Even I don't understand it. Your dad was married to my mother, but he's not my dad, and your mum isn't related to me." She held up her hands. "But, my mother is your godmother, so I think we're like half-sisters."

Isabelle nodded. "Except we're *not* half-sisters at all."

Elizabeth giggled. "I mean," she said, "what's hard to understand about that?"

Isabelle wanted to stay gloomy but her laugh was infectious, and soon she found herself laughing, too.

"It's perfectly clear," she agreed.

Raj shook his head and muttered, "Rich people are crazy."

"I would argue, but it's true," Elizabeth wiped tears from the corner of her eyes, careful not smear her thick eyeliner. "Especially our family."

Isabelle leaned back to study her. "Why is your make-up always perfect? And what is that eye pencil colour? It's like purple but it's not purple."

Elizabeth brightened as the topic strayed to her second favourite subject. "It's called plum brandy. I picked it up at Selfridges at half term…"

"Well, that's my cue." Raj took a step back, holding up his hands. "When they start talking about make-up it's time to go play football."

"Wait. We'll talk about something else!" Isabelle backtracked instantly, but he was already turning to walk away. "The game awaits," he said, waving over his shoulder. "Catch you at dinner."

Disappointed, she watched as he melted into the crowd. He had such a distinctive way of moving – steps light and smooth on the battered oak floor. She wondered where he'd learned to walk like that. He'd once told her his father was a hard man to live with. Maybe he'd moved quietly all his life to avoid being noticed.

Elizabeth nudged her shoulder. "You fancy the pants off him."

"I do *not*," Isabelle insisted, colour creeping up her neck to her cheeks.

"Oh, please. You fancy him *so much*. And I don't blame you. He gets hotter every year. He's got the nicest bum." She made an apple shape with her hands. "All muscle."

"*Elizabeth.*"

Her half-sister's wicked smile didn't waver. "When are you going to make your move?"

"Oh, don't be gross." Isabelle rolled her eyes. "What do you even mean, 'make my move'?"

Elizabeth didn't miss a beat. "I mean seduce him, of course."

For a second, Isabelle couldn't find words. "What? This isn't *Dynasty*. I'm not seducing anyone."

"Why not?" The other girl seemed genuinely baffled. "You fancy him. You're both young and single and free. You just have to let him know you're interested."

In truth, Isabelle had no idea how to seduce anyone. It seemed like something older women did, while wearing jackets with shoulder pads and oversized jewellery. It wasn't something girls her age did.

"I don't think he's interested," she said, glancing away. "I don't blame him." She plucked at the unflattering pleats of her skirt. "I'm so ordinary compared to most of the girls here."

Elizabeth's brow furrowed. "Don't be ridiculous. You're gorgeous. Your bone structure is deadly. I'd bloody kill for your cheekbones. You just don't make yourself up. You need to do something to stand out. Get him to notice you as more than one of the guys."

Isabelle's hand drifted up to her face and then fell again. She didn't know good cheekbones from bad. She didn't know how to fix everything that was wrong with her. All she knew was she'd had a crush on Raj Patel for two years now and he was more interested in kicking a football than in her.

"I've tried everything I can think of," she confessed, miserably. "But he thinks of me as a friend."

"He probably says the same thing about you." Elizabeth sighed. "You're both impossible. You obviously like each other, but neither of you will do anything about it."

"I don't know how to do the things you do." Isabelle gestured at Elizabeth's shortened skirt, and perfectly fluffed hair. "I don't know how to get boys' attention."

"Come on, it isn't science." Tilting her head, Elizabeth studied her, tapping her cheek with one finger. "Or maybe it is. Do you know what? If make-up will give you confidence, I can loan you some. I've got the perfect eyeliner for you. And your hair would look so much better with a little mousse." She was warming to the topic, her eyes skating across Isabelle's face as if she could already see the transformation. "Let me fix you up."

"I don't know," Isabelle said. "I just don't think I'm cut out for the seduction stuff."

"Of course, you are." Elizabeth dismissed this with a wave of her hand. "I'll bring some stuff to your room later and we can try it on. If you don't like it, you can take it right off again." Isabelle opened her mouth to argue, but Elizabeth kept going. "You know, you only get to be wild and pretty once in your life. What you don't want is to be wild later when it's just too tragic. You need to do it now, while you're young and cool." She put a hand on her hip and turned the full power of her smile on a group of younger boys passing by. Two of them stumbled as they stared at her. "See?" She turned back to Isabelle. "It's all in the confidence. All you need is a little faith in yourself, and Raj will tumble at your feet."

That didn't seem possible, but there was no point in arguing once she had her mind made up. Instead, Isabelle asked, "Why do you care so much if we get together?"

"I don't. All I'm saying is, he's a good choice for you," Elizabeth said. "He's smart. He's super cute. Also, he doesn't seem like the type to go after your money."

Isabelle's smile faded. She stared at her friend as if she'd suddenly stopped speaking English. "Of course he isn't after money. What an odd thing to say."

"Don't 'of course' me. You have to think about stuff like that." Turning to the mirror, Elizabeth examined herself, swishing her hair with the tips of her fingers. "You're going to be worth millions someday. The stock market crashed a few months ago and somehow your dad made money off of that. I heard Lucinda's financial advisor tell her the trust fund your dad set up for her skyrocketed." Lucinda was her mother. For reasons Isabelle didn't fully understand, she never called her "mum".

"Every guy in this school who lost his trust fund is going to be sniffing around both of us before too long," Elizabeth continued. "But Raj … he strikes me as someone who doesn't care that much about money."

Her tone was mild, as if she were talking about a school assignment, but her words rocked Isabelle. It had never occurred to her that she would have money of her own, or that anyone would pretend to like her in order to have that money for himself. But her father was Alastair St John. Everyone knew he was one of the richest men in the country. Aside from a few scholarship students, everyone at Cimmeria came from money, but not like her family. Her father had made multiple fortunes – everything he touched really did turn to gold, and he donated regularly to the school. This mattered. Even the teachers treated her with more deference than other students. Hollis had forgiven her immediately for skipping class last week. She hadn't even been given detention. Elizabeth broke the rules constantly, and all the teachers treated her like a perfect student.

And Raj had alluded to it that afternoon, hadn't he? *You could get away with murder here.*

Still, Elizabeth was wrong – she wasn't going to be her father's heir. There was someone else in line for that.

"I don't think I'll inherit that much," she said, after a second. "Nathaniel will get it. Everyone knows that."

"Maybe." Elizabeth gave her a meaningful look. "Or, maybe not."

Isabelle was confused. Her half-brother Nathaniel was two years older than her, and a boy. It would be normal for him to inherit the bulk of their father's estate.

"Why wouldn't he get everything?" she asked.

"I don't know." Still looking in the mirror, Elizabeth pulled a lipstick from her pocket and began painting her lips a deep raspberry shade. "All I know is, Lucinda says she has a feeling he won't."

"But if *he* doesn't get the money…" Isabelle began. Elizabeth finished the sentence for her.

"You will." Closing the lipstick with a decisive click, she dropped it into the pocket of her navy blazer. "You're his only other child. And according to Lucinda, his favourite." The Cimmeria crest on Elizabeth's lapel gleamed white against the dark fabric when she leaned back against the marble table.

"But…" Isabelle was still frowning, "that doesn't make sense. Why me?"

"I'm not sure your dad likes Nathaniel that much. Lucinda's always going on about it. She's really much more interested in him than she is in me." She glanced at her watch. "Right. I need to bail. I'm supposed to meet Aaron at the chapel for some illicit lip action."

Isabelle said nothing. Her mind was tangled up in the bombshell that had just dropped on her. Her mother and her father had stayed close after their divorce. She'd recently remarried, to a wealthy financier. He was nice enough on the rare occasions when Isabelle met him, and her mother seemed happy, and that was what mattered. Although she missed Scotland – after she married, her mother had sold the house outside Edinburgh. Now, she and her new husband split their time between London and a country estate in Hampshire. Nobody, of course, had asked Isabelle what she wanted. But then, she mostly lived here these days.

Elizabeth started to walk away but she turned back abruptly. "Oh hey. There's a bonfire up at the castle tonight after curfew. You should come." Isabelle had already begun to shake her head when she added, "Raj'll be there. I'll come by your room after dinner and do your make-up. You can dazzle him." She gave a dangerous smile. "If you don't come and claim him though – beware. I might get there first."

Everything looked
normal, but the night felt
electric. As if it waited
for something it knew
that she didn't.

Night School 1987

– PART 2 –

That night, Isabelle left her room just before midnight.

The mirror by the door reflected a face that was almost unrecognisable as her own. True to her promise, Elizabeth had come by after dinner with her pockets full of cosmetics. With her boombox in the corner of the room blasting Whitney Houston singing "I want to dance with somebody…" full blast, she'd sat her down and shown her how to line her eyes with pencil, shadow her lids, and highlight her lashes with mascara.

"All you need," she'd said, brushing bronzer on Isabelle's cheeks, "is to bring out your best parts." When she'd finished, she'd leaned back and smiled.

"I mean. I *am* good. If Raj doesn't notice you now, he needs glasses."

Isabelle looked more like the glitter girls now. Her unusual amber eyes seemed suddenly dramatic and huge surrounded by eye liner. She'd never really noticed her lips before but suddenly they seemed weirdly obvious. Her untameable hair for once was almost under control, but it had grown to twice its normal size after Elizabeth made her turn her head upside down and squeeze mousse into the waves.

"I look like a backup singer for Wham," she muttered to herself. But she didn't try to rub any of the make-up off, either. If this was what it took to get Raj's attention, then she'd try it.

She'd puzzled endlessly over what to wear but the school gave her few choices. There was no point in keeping her uniform on, so she'd changed into the stretch leggings she wore for P.E. with ankle boots and an oversized white blouse. She wore a light blazer she'd brought from home over the shirt and big, silver hoop earrings to catch the light. When she'd finished, she spritzed herself with the Halston perfume her mother had given to her for her birthday.

If nothing else, she looked (and smelled) more interesting than usual.

She wasn't sure why she was trying so hard, it was just that something told her tonight mattered. There was a now-or-never feel about this party.

Something Elizabeth had said before she left had really resonated. After Isabelle was polished, she'd lingered in the doorway.

"You know, Izzy, Raj's a good guy, but it's entirely possible that he doesn't deserve you."

Isabelle had been so shocked it had taken her a moment to reply. "What do you mean?"

"It's just, you're *you*. You're pretty and smart and rich." She held up a hand in anticipation of Isabelle's objections. "I know you don't think that should matter, but it matters. You have everything to offer. If he doesn't see it, you deserve better. There are some great guys out there. Find one who appreciates you. OK?"

There'd been a hint of pity in Elizabeth's voice, and that was the worst part. Isabelle wanted to defend herself, but the truth was, she'd waited years for Raj to notice her. Everyone knew she had a crush on him, and he simply ignored it.

Elizabeth was right. At some point, she had to give up on him as anything more than a friend.

The worst part of love, she was learning, was that she couldn't make someone love her back. But by God, she could *try*.

"Here goes nothing," she told herself. She slipped off her boots and, holding them in one hand stepped out of the room, closing the door behind her softly.

The narrow hallway was hushed and dark – most of the lights were burned out and no one had bothered to replace them – but she knew the school so well she didn't need to see her way as she tiptoed in her socks past dozens of small doors just like hers, each with a number painted in glossy black. At the end of the corridor, she hurried down a narrow staircase to the first-floor landing, where a row of marble statues were ghostly in the moonlight. She tried not to look at them as she raced across to the curved main staircase and started down. There was something about them that gave her the creeps. They were too expressive. When she was younger she'd convinced herself they shifted position whenever her back was turned in order to watch her more closely. She was too old to believe that anymore. And yet...

She'd just reached the bottom step when something creaked above her head.

She froze, one hand tight on the worn oak bannister, and looked up. The moonlight through the tall windows sent shadows chasing around the statues, giving the illusion that they swayed and shifted in the dark.

Goosebumps rose on the backs of her arms. She loved Cimmeria, but with the spiderwebs and the cracked windows, the way the pipes constantly made sounds uncannily like a person was walking through the walls, the place was bloody scary at night.

She could have kicked herself for not going out at the same time as Elizabeth. But she hadn't been convinced until the last few minutes that she was really going to go at all. Everyone else had already been up at the castle for nearly an hour.

Stupid indecision, she thought as she squinted into the darkness.

She couldn't see anyone above her. And nothing stirred from the teachers' dorm wing, just across the atrium from where she stood now.

Maybe she'd imagined it.

She released her grip on the banister, and took the last step to the ground. The second she did, a loud – *bang!* – split the quiet, from somewhere above. Something falling, or being pushed. Whatever had made that sound, she didn't want to know.

She took off, skidding in her socks as she hurtled to the wide hallway, past the dining hall and the common room, uncannily quiet at this hour, and then to the entrance hall where the floor turned to old, soft stone, stopping only when she slid up to the tall, arched front door. Blackened with soot and time, it was thought to be as old as the school itself. The lock mechanism was ancient, a heavy, iron device that involved (she knew from past experience) pulling a latch at the top while also turning a knob beneath it, and then heaving it open without letting go of either.

She tucked her boots under one arm and grabbed the lock but her hands were slick with nervousness and couldn't seem to grip; her fingers slipped from the latch three times before she finally got a good hold on it and wrenched the door open.

Cool night air flowed in, heavy with the English summer scent of pine needles, cut grass and night flowers. Without looking back, she threw herself outside and spun around to push the door to. The clunk of the latch sealing seemed far too loud in the quiet.

She dashed down the stone steps to the drive that curved in front of the school like a question mark. The gravel was small, cold knives curtting into her feet and she hopped on one foot and then the other as she pulled her ankle boots back on.

When she was finished, she looked around. A fine, warm breath of excitement ran through her. It was nearly midnight and yet she felt wide awake. Exhilarated. Overhead, the moon was full, and shone down on the school with the power of a hundred spotlights. She could make out every red Victorian brick in its glow. See the steep peaks of the old roof. The jutting points of the chimneys. The glow of light in the few windows on the top floor where students were still awake. And ahead, the path curving around the building to the forest, and beyond that the hill leading up to the old castle at the top.

Anticipation tightened her ribs around her lungs and she wanted to laugh for some reason. She wasn't one for breaking the Rules but it was just as well that she'd come out tonight. She couldn't have slept anyway. Not with the moon like that.

A bird flapped across the sky, sending its shadow soft along the grass, a brush of darkness on the green. The sight of it galvanised her.

Setting her shoulders, she ran along the edge of the gravel, where her steps would be less noisy, her stride long and confident, until she'd passed the classroom wing and joined the footpath that led through the trees. Only then did she slow down to a fast walk.

She'd forgotten to bring a flashlight, but she didn't need one. The moon lit up the grounds so clearly she could see the pine needles on the branches – tiny, jagged, and clear. To her left, the ghostly white dome of the folly rose above the trees.

Everything looked normal, but the night felt electric. As if it waited for something it knew that she didn't. Something that was about to happen.

"I'm losing it," she whispered to herself. She wasn't the kind to *feel* things in the air. She was rational. She didn't believe in horoscopes or Magic 8 balls. She didn't want her fortune read. Nothing much scared her. She was completely focussed on being the top in her class, and everything else, she'd always believed, was just pointless distraction.

That was why she didn't usually come to these parties. She had a plan for her life, and it did not include alcohol or detention or, for that matter, inheriting her father's money. She'd never have told Elizabeth – because she knew she'd laugh at her – but, she didn't want any of that. She wanted to follow in her godmother's footsteps. She wanted to sit on the board of directors like Lucinda with all those men, and prove that a woman could do anything they could do. She wanted to run a company that gave a lot of people good jobs, and made their lives better. Most of all, she wanted to be a member of Parliament. Then she could change unfair laws. She'd grown up aware of the constant protests in the country over things the government was doing. If that many people were upset enough to fight the police over it, something was wrong. And she wanted to fix it.

Elizabeth always told her that she was wasting her youth. And maybe she was. But she didn't really think so. She thought she was using it to get herself ready to change the world.

That's what she should be doing now, she told herself. She should be in her room preparing for the next day's lessons, instead of chasing after boys.

She suddenly became aware that it had grown darker. She looked around, surprised to see that while she'd been lost in thought, she'd entered the woods and begun the climb up the hill. The branches of the tall Scotch pines stretched out above her head, forming a tunnel that blocked the moonlight.

She hurried her pace, trying not to look too hard into the shadows under the trees. She thought of the others, already up at the castle, sitting around the fire drinking wine they'd pilfered from the cellars the teachers thought they didn't know about, or the gin they'd sneaked into their luggage. She wanted to be there now.

That was when she heard footsteps behind her, steady but approaching quickly. She drew in a breath. Someone else must be late. She could walk with them.

And yet, she didn't slow down. The footsteps stayed behind her, steady and keeping pace.

"Hello?" she called into the darkness, her voice hesitant.

Nobody answered.

Shivering, she pulled her jacket tighter across her shoulders and broke into a jog.

Instantly, the footsteps sped up. Whoever it was, they were following her.

Isabelle shot a glance over her shoulder but could see only darkness. But the footsteps seemed to be keeping pace with hers.

She knew sound carried strangely in the woods. The person could have been further away from her than it sounded.

Or, a voice in her head whispered, *closer*.

Already winded from the uphill run, she made herself move faster, hoping she'd hear nothing else. No footsteps. No one there.

But, behind her, the unseen person also sped up. She could hear the footsteps more clearly now, fast but uneven, a piece of gravel skidding under a poorly placed heel.

For the first time, she grew genuinely nervous. Someone was definitely following her. Who would do that? Who even knew she was here?

She thought of what Elizabeth had said earlier, about people wanting her money, knowing her family was rich. If boys knew it, other people could know it, too. Strangers could know it. She felt exposed — as if all her secrets had been revealed.

In seconds, she found herself sprinting up the path. She didn't know why she was doing it. Nothing ever happened here — it was perfectly safe. The school wasn't fenced or gated, but the driveway was marked "private" and it was two miles from the nearest road to the actual school building. All of a sudden, though, that didn't seem like enough.

Why isn't there a fence? Why aren't we better protected? she wondered wildly as she flew up the hill, heedless of the uneven path. *We need more security. We need guards...*

"Isabelle! Wait!" the voice came from behind her. Male. With a faint Scottish burr.

Her steps slowed, and she turned back, breathless, just as Nathaniel melted out of the darkness behind her. She was instantly embarrassed.

"Oh, it's you," she said, pausing to wait for him.

He stopped a short distance away, his hands shoved deep into his pockets, a wary, almost wounded, look on his fine-boned face. "Why did you run?"

It was so like him to scare her half to death and then take offense because she was frightened.

"I didn't know it was you," she said, adding, as explanation, "It's dark."

"I wasn't sure it was you at first either. I didn't expect you to be here," he said. "You don't usually go to these things."

"You don't either," she reminded him. "Or, at least, I thought you didn't."

"Not normally," he agreed. "But tonight I just felt like, I don't know." He hunched his shoulders, kicking a rock off the path into the ferns. "Something different."

It was so weird that he now seemed to want to have a conversation on a hillside in the dark, while also acting as if every word was excruciating.

Why is he so odd? she wondered.

"I couldn't sleep either." She gestured to the glow filtering through the long tree branches above them. "It's the moon."

He glanced up, blankly. "What does the moon have to do with it?"

"It's scientifically proven that a full moon affects human behaviour," she informed him. "More crimes are committed on nights when there's a full moon. And more people die."

He made a bored face. "I've never believed that moon stuff. I mean, how can it hurt us? It's just a rock."

As he spoke, he glanced up at her. They had different mothers but it occurred to her for the first time that no one would have been shocked to find out they were related. They shared their father's high cheekbones, strong chin, and golden brown hair. The main difference was in the eyes. She had her mother's strange amber eyes, while he had their father's narrow blue gaze.

"Rocks can hurt," she replied, tartly. "I mean, if they hit you hard enough."

He barked a short laugh. "Well, I can't argue with that."

This seemed to break the ice, and the two of them began walking up the hill together. Isabelle struggled to think of something to fill the silence. She kept hearing Elizabeth's voice saying *I'm not sure your dad likes Nathaniel that much*, and it felt like betrayal to even remember that. Because as soon as she'd said it she knew it was true. It had always been evident their father didn't much like his only son. He sent him away as soon as he could, and spent as little time with him as possible. Nathaniel had been desperate for a parent to care for him, and in the end, Lucinda had been the one to give him that affection. But it was his father he wanted.

His mother had died when he was very young – he'd been raised primarily by nannies. When Isabelle was a child, Nathaniel had been around, a skinny, sad-eyed boy, always playing alone. They'd struck up a sort of friendship when she was old enough to play, but she was just that little bit too young to be a proper playmate. There had, though, been one fleeting moment when they could have formed a closer friendship. When she was five and he was seven, she was old enough to be interesting to him. They'd spent that summer running around the grounds of the Scottish mansion where their father lived. Nathaniel had involved her in his games – searching for pirates on the pond, hunting for treasure beneath the trees.

But within weeks Nathaniel turned eight, and his father sent him away to boarding school. After that, she didn't see him much. He'd come home in the summer for a few weeks, almost unrecognisable for how much he'd grown and changed. They would talk a little, but whatever family connection they'd formed during those hazy warm months was over. He was introverted and tended to keep to himself. Her smiles were not returned.

And then her parents had divorced and after that she scarcely saw him at all.

She was twelve when she came to Cimmeria, and by then he was fourteen, and the gap between them seemed vast. He showed little interest in renewing any sort of family friendship. He was polite but not at all warm. And it seemed to her the only thing to do was to keep her distance.

She'd always felt a little sad that they weren't closer – she and Elizabeth had been friends from the start. But Nathaniel cultivated his outsider status. As far as she could tell, he had few friends. He wanted people to keep their distance, and they did.

Gradually, the silence grew heavy and she found herself becoming paranoid that somehow he knew all the things she wasn't saying.

Say something, she urged herself, silently. *Anything but that.*

"It must be weird for you." The words burst out of her too loudly, and he gave her a strange look. She hurried to explain, "I mean, it's your last year at Cimmeria. Your last bonfires at the castle, and all of that."

"Honestly? I can't wait to get out of here." The venom in his tone took her by surprise and she blinked at him as he continued. "I despise this place. The head should have retired a decade ago – half the teachers are past retirement age, they can barely stay awake long enough to teach one lesson. The building is crumbling around our ears, the grounds are overgrown." He waved a hand at the trees around them as if they, too, were inadequate. "It's a terrible school. I've wasted years here. Years. All because our father has some obsession with the place. No, I have no regrets about leaving. I'd go today if I could."

"But, you must have friends here?" she tried, with caution. "Surely you'll miss them."

He gave a dismissive laugh. "Who would I be friends with here? At Eton or Harrow I might have made friends. But Father insisted I go here." His tone was arrogant, but there was something beneath it. A kind of sorrow. Isabelle wondered if he knew all the things Elizabeth had said. If he knew his father didn't like him. And if it made him feel more alone.

Abruptly, he turned his gaze to her. "But you like it here, don't you?" It sounded like an accusation.

"I guess. I mean. I see what you mean – the teachers are a bit old, and the building needs work. But..." She looked down to where ferns reached out soft fronds from the sides of the path to brush against her legs. "...There's something about it."

"Something toxic," he muttered.

"I wish someone would fix it up," she said, ignoring that. "Give it the care it deserves."

Through a parting in the trees she spotted a faint glow lighting up the horizon. She could smell a whiff of sweet wood smoke on the breeze. Relief spread through her. "Oh look! The bonfire. We're nearly there."

Nathaniel's lip curled as if the bonfire were another ridiculous Cimmeria affectation. He lingered on the path, but she didn't wait for him, half-running across the top of the hill to the old stone wall that surrounded the ruined fortress. She clambered across the rocks without looking back. A group of about twenty people were gathered around a blazing fire. Almost immediately, Elizabeth spotted her and jumped to her feet.

"I was starting to think you weren't coming!" Her cheeks were flushed from whatever was sloshing in the plastic cup she held as she grabbed Isabelle's hand and pulled her toward the fire. "Caroline's going to teach us how to make s'mores!"

Caroline was an American exchange student who'd arrived that autumn, bringing curious phrases, weird music, and copies of *Rolling Stone* magazine with her that the students passed around like contraband.

Isabelle started to follow her but then, remembering Nathaniel was behind her, she turned back. "Come with us..."

There was no one there.

At some point, he'd melted away as suddenly as he'd arrived.

"Who are you talking to?" Elizabeth peered into the shadows behind her and, seeing no one, poked her playfully in the shoulder. "You're talking to pretend people."

Her eyes were too bright and she slurred her words slightly. Isabelle realised she might be properly drunk.

Forcing a smile, she shrugged. "My imaginary friends are my best friends. Hey, I think you're wasted, by the way."

Elizabeth beamed a wide smile at her. "Tristram made punch, and the boys brought it up here in an actual bucket. It's delicious."

Taking the cup from her, Isabelle sniffed it doubtfully. Her nose wrinkled. "It's nearly pure alcohol. You should take it easy with this."

Elizabeth shrugged and snatched the cup back and took a deep drink. "Getting my money's worth."

Isabelle watched with concern as her half-sister tottered unsteadily back to the crowd. She followed at a distance, careful where she walked. The remnants of the castle were limited to an old keep – its windows, roof, and doors were long gone, but the round sturdy shape of it was still solidly in place. The rest had been broken up over time, and chunks of ancient masonry lay scattered on the ground.

When they reached the others, Elizabeth reached back for her hand and dragged her down to sit on a large stone with her.

As she joined the group, Isabelle eagerly scanned their faces, but there was no sign of Raj.

"Hey," she said casually, "have you seen Raj."

Elizabeth gave her a shifty look. "Yeah, there's something I need to tell you." She pulled Isabelle closer, but grabbed her too hard, nearly knocking her over. Isabelle had to hold onto the stone they sat on to keep from falling over. Elizabeth leaned her head towards hers. "He's here," she stage whispered. "But he's not alone." Her breath smelled of vodka and some overly sweet fruit juice.

Isabelle searched her eyes. Willing her to be sober enough to explain.

Elizabeth darted a significant look at the castle keep. "He's with Caroline."

Isabelle's heart sank. The castle was where couples went to make out without being seen.

"Oh," she said, quietly.

Elizabeth shook her head and took another drink from the cup. "I tried'a tell him, Izzy. But he wouldn't listen. He's a wanker. A complete wanker. You're better off without him."

Isabelle kept her eyes on her boots as heat flooded her face. This was worse than she'd dared to imagine. Elizabeth, drunk and determined, must have told Raj she liked him. So now, he knew the truth, and he was off making out with blonde, suntanned, Californian Caroline. Bringer of s'mores.

"Fabulous," she breathed to her boots, as if they alone understood her pain.

Sensing her mood drop even through the haze of booze, Elizabeth picked up a long stick and held it out to her, hopefully.

"We're goin'a moast rarshmellows," she explained. She paused to stare at the stick blankly, before beginning to giggle. "Other way round."

Isabelle lifted her head to stare at her. She was always a little wild, but she'd never seen her half-sister this drunk.

"She's been drinking like a fish all night." The cut glass voice came from her elbow, and she turned as flickering firelight illuminated the blonde hair and distinctive, aristocratic face of Julian le Fanult. "Everyone has. It's been like a party at the end of the world."

"Why didn't anyone stop her?" Isabelle demanded, glancing at Elizabeth, who was struggling to pierce a marshmallow onto the end of the long stick.

His eyebrows winged up. "Have you ever tried to stop Elizabeth Meldrum from doing precisely what she wants? It's like trying to stop a river from running to the sea."

"But, look at her," Isabelle gestured to where the other girl was now studying the marshmallow in the firelight and whispering to it. "How are we going to get her back in the school?"

"I've been thinking about this for a while," Julian said. "I'm starting to accept that this is just one of those nights where everyone needs to save themselves and everyone else be damned. I suggest we deposit her safely in the common room, covered in a blanket, and then slip back to our rooms, so that when Fergie finds half the senior students unconscious in the morning, we will be snuggled angelically in bed. Sober as vicars."

Despite her worry about Elizabeth, Isabelle found herself smiling. She'd always liked Julian. He was quiet, but when he spoke he was often devastatingly funny, or quietly cutting. It was an admirable skill.

"I can't leave her, though," she reminded him. "She's almost my sister."

"Who is?" Elizabeth blinked at her. "Oh, me!" She seemed pleased by this discovery. "Who're you talking to?" She leaned across Isabelle's lap to peer at Julian. "Oh it's you! You're so cute." She shook her finger at him, her elbow digging into Isabelle's leg. "You like Isabelle but don't even try. She's in love with Raj." She waved her hand back and forth between them. "Star-crossed! Star-crossed."

Isabelle had had enough. She plucked the plastic cup from Elizabeth's hand and dumped the contents on the ground.

"And that's enough booze for you," she announced, pushing Elizabeth off her lap and standing up as the other girl began to protest. "We are going back. You're too wasted. I'm getting you into bed before you pass out."

Julian stood up to join her. At more than six feet tall, he towered over her. "Let me assist you." His patrician face showed no evidence that he'd heard anything Elizabeth had said seconds ago, even though he must have.

Clinging to her roasting stick, a marshmallow dangling from one end, she glared at the two of them. "What are you, the Stasi? I jus' got here, an I'm stayin'."

"I don't think so." Julian stood next to Isabelle. Glancing at the rest of the group he announced, "Drink up, losers. It's nearly one. We're all about to turn into pumpkins."

The others grumbled, but began to shuffle, as if they knew he was right.

There was something authoritative about Julian, Isabelle thought. Something that made people listen. She could learn from that. Use it herself.

From the corner of her eye, she noticed two people stumble out of the castle keep. She saw Raj's dark head, and Caroline's long, blonde hair catching the light of the fire and turning to gold. He had his arm around her shoulders, and she was holding onto his hand. Isabelle only caught a glimpse, but they looked happy.

Ignoring the ice forming deep in her stomach, she forced herself to focus on getting Elizabeth to her feet.

"Come on, Lizzie," she cajoled, pulling her up. "We have to go. It's late."

"Jus' got here," Elizabeth objected, but she dropped the stick and climbed unsteadily to her feet.

"Right." Julian took Elizabeth's left elbow. Isabelle put her arm around her waist from the other side, and they began heading across the ruins towards the footpath.

"I wanna stay!" Elizabeth protested, trying to turn back. But they held her firmly and kept her moving towards the safety of the school.

"This is not the night I was expecting," Isabelle said, mostly to herself.

Over the top of Elizabeth's head, Julian gave her an enigmatic smile. "That's the thing about bonfires. They're always a little weird."

Did he really like her? Elizabeth was a pain but she was rarely wrong about this sort of thing. And if he did, had it been him she was thinking about earlier tonight when she told Isabelle not to wait for Raj.

It puzzled her that she hadn't noticed before that Julian was interested. But then, he was the type to find it very easy to hide his emotions.

Isabelle wondered if she could like him as much as she liked Raj. She hoped so.

Because she was tired of being ignored.

For a while, they were busy navigating Elizabeth through the opening in the stone wall and down the path. Away from the warmth of the fire and the constant flow of booze, she'd quickly begun to fall asleep, so it was mostly a matter of keeping her upright and moving.

"She's small to be so heavy," Julian observed, glancing down at her.

Isabelle, panting from the exertion of holding her up said, "She'd kill you if she heard you say that."

This made him laugh. "If she ever finds out I know who to blame."

There was a brief pause as they followed the path through the trees, where the dappled moonlight formed elaborate patterns on the forest floor.

"It's a shame you didn't come earlier," Julian said, looking ahead. "Elizabeth may be drunk but she was right about one thing – I did mean to ask you out."

So he had heard.

"Did you?"

"Yes. I've been planning it for ages. I thought, well, hoped the moonlight might work in my favour. Romance and all."

Heat rose to her cheeks, and she was glad of the darkness.

She wasn't sure what to do. She loved someone else. But here was a tall, thoughtful boy openly confessing that he was interested. Saying everything Raj had never said.

Maybe, the time comes when waiting has to end, so something new can start.

She cleared her throat. "Well, here we are in the romantic moonlight," she said, shifting her grip on Elizabeth's waist. "You should ask me."

In the pale blue light, she saw his lips curve up. "Isabelle," he said, "would you go out with me?"

"I'd love to," she said, pushing every thought of Raj out of her mind.

"'Zis iz beautiful," Elizabeth murmured, through her hair.

"It would be the perfect time to kiss you but…" Julian gestured at her with his free hand. Their laughter hid the sound of footsteps, so they both jumped when Nathaniel thundered out of the shadows toward them. He was coming from the direction of the school below.

Isabelle was confounded – the last time she'd seen him he'd been at the edge of the bonfire. Now, he looked strange, drawn and pale, every muscle in his body strung tight as a wire.

"What—" she began but he spoke over her. "Isabelle, we have to get home," he said. "Now."

His eyes were intense, fixed on her. He didn't even seem to notice the presence of Julian or Elizabeth, slumped in between them.

She stared at him, baffled. "I'm sorry, I don't understand… Home?"

"Something's happened." Somehow he imbued those words with such ominous meaning she found her hands slipping away from her half-sister.

Julian stood still, holding the semi-conscious Elizabeth upright and watching Nathaniel as carefully as you would observe a snake.

"Nathaniel." Isabelle's voice took on the preternatural calm note she always adopted when she was afraid. "Is it mum? Is she hurt? Tell me now."

Elizabeth, perhaps sensing through the haze of booze, the trouble in the air, mumbled worriedly, but Isabelle didn't look at her. She was watching Nathaniel. He was trembling.

"It's not her," he said, clearly struggling to find the words. "It's father." He drew a breath, hands clenching at his sides.

"His plane is missing."

Night School, With Vampires

As you already know if you subscribe to my YouTube channel (and if you don't, why don't you?), in its earliest versions, Night School was a paranormal book. In it, the students were mostly vampires, known as 'Eternals'. This was the secret the school was protecting. And Allie's secret, the one that neither she, nor anyone at the school knew when she first arrived, was that she was a witch.

Goddess above, I loved it. I loved the vampires and their wicked ways. I loved Allie's accidental witchiness. I loved all of it. The only problem was, everyone told me it was too late. Publishing had had enough of vampires. Editors and agents were bored of witches. No one would publish the book unless I came up with another idea. Somehow, I had to make it non-paranormal

Faced with that kind of feedback, I did what any writer desperate to get her first book published would do – I killed the vampires. But I have always wondered if they were wrong.

Honestly, I think it was a good book with vampires. And it would have been an amazing series. It would have been *very* different from the Night School we know, of course. But I would have written that book eventually.

Still, life happens. Reality bites. And Night School as we know and love it happened. I regret nothing. But the Eternals are still there, in the back of my mind. And their story has never been seen. Until now.

So here, exclusively, is an extended excerpt of the original Night School. You are the first in the world to read it.

The excerpt begins near the end of the book. The school is about to be attacked by Nathaniel and his gang of vampires. He doesn't know the students have been training for this. So everyone's in for a surprise.

Things you need to know: They all have weapons. Allie and Carter have discovered they can communicate without talking. Allie can shut a door in her mind to keep him (and others) out. Carter can "see" things happening far away. Eternals have all kinds of crazy powers.

Oh yeah, and there's a ghost in the library.

Welcome to Night School, as it might have been.

She took a tentative

step to the left. This

time the voice was

clearer. "Yes".

Chapter Twenty

"Ow! Bloody hell."

Allie, rushing down the stairs, winced as her weapon bag hit her hard on the thigh.

How does anybody run or fight with this thing on? More to the point: how will I?

It was nearly eleven and she was only just now awake and out of her room. They'd been up talking and planning until five so she didn't feel guilty about being late; she just wondered what she'd missed.

Walking down the empty hall, she peeked into the dining room hoping for breakfast leftovers, but found it empty.

In the library she made her way around stacks of moulded body armour that appeared to be made of black plastic ("Cool stuff," Carter would explain later. "Like Kevlar, only better."). Piles of weaponry dominated the room, and students sat alone or in clusters, talking and resting.

A flash of colour caught her eye, and she turned to see boxes of power bars stacked alongside vivid rows of bright blue and green energy drinks.

"Awesome," she murmured as she grabbed one of each, and looked around the room for friendly faces.

Rachel was in a corner organising plastic bags. Allie ambled over, ripping open a power bar.

"What's all that stuff?" she mumbled through a mouthful of bar.

"Bandages," Rachel replied brightly. She made a rolling motion with her right hand. "And tourniquets and other stuff. How are you?"

Allie swallowed hard.

"Fine," she said, looking at the stacks of bags. "Rachel, how many bandages do you think we'll need?"

"However many we need, I'm ready." She looked serious. "Most of the nursing staff are gone now but, don't worry. We'll be fine. Jo will help and so can you. We'll be fine."

"Yeah. You said that already," Allie said, bemused. She changed the subject while trying to open her drink with one hand. "How long have you been up? Has anything been happening?"

Rachel wrinkled her nose with concentration as she made a note on her clipboard. "Oh, I didn't go to sleep at all in the end. We don't actually need to sleep much, to be honest, so I used the time to get ready. It was kind of fun.

"I found the food in the kitchen cupboard," she said gesturing at the power bars. She smiled modestly. "Everybody thought I was a hero."

"Well spotted," Allie said, toasting her with her bottle. "I'm starving."

Rachel ticked off the latest news. "Nothing happened while you slept. Isabelle's locked up with Matthew – that's the guy she brought to the ball, remember him? Kind of weird? Bit intense? – and a few teachers. Mr Ellison is going around doing some hocus-pocus to try and make the building more secure, if you believe in that sort of thing. Which I don't."

Allie lowered her voice conspiratorially. "What is Mr Ellison anyway? You don't buy it? I was wondering why, if he could protect one room, he doesn't just do the whole school. I mean, why just have the world's safest library?"

Rachel looked around to make sure nobody could overhear. "I don't entirely understand it, to be honest. It's just superstition. I don't believe this room is safe. Shaking some herbs around isn't going to make a bit of difference. But Isabelle says it's tradition before any battle, that they've always done it, it's like the blessing of the fleet, blah blah blah."

Allie felt like she should defend Mr Ellison, but at the same time, she didn't believe in magic herself. Yes, she had been sleeping incredibly well since his visit, but that was due to exhaustion. Not magic.

"Well, what harm can it do? And he seems really nice," she said loyally.

"He does seem nice," Rachel conceded with a shrug.

"So… What happens now?" Allie asked.

Rachel straightened an already straight row of bandages. "Now, we wait. Everything's ready."

***

Last night's excitement evaporated in the light of day. As the day progressed the students were increasingly sombre and tense. Most of the Night School students sat alone, staring into space. Allie helped where she could, but there was little left to do. Ultimately she began making up ways to stay busy, and by five o'clock she was sitting on the floor between two rows of shelves, pulling books off at random. It was an old game she'd played as a child. She closed her eyes, flipped to a page, pointed at a line, then opened her eyes again to see what word she'd chosen.

If the word or phrase were appropriate to the circumstances in which she found herself, it was a portent. If she was about to go on a car journey, for example, and her finger alighted on 'crash' (never happened) she would refuse to go. Usually, of course, her finger fell on something like 'octopus' or 'quintuplets'.

So far, as most of the books she'd opened had proven not to be in English, she had no idea what words she'd chosen. Now, she had chosen a stack of books in a language she could understand and was preparing to begin again.

Twice she'd heard an odd rustling noise above her head and looked up to find nothing there. She remembered the day she'd been alone here and books had rained down on her head.

"Not right now, mister ghost," she sniped at the stacks, before returning to her game. "I'm busy."

In the first book her finger pointed at the word 'ambition'.

Could be significant.

She set that book down and opened the next.

'Valise'.

Random.

133

She slapped the book shut and pushed it aside. As she reached behind for another volume, a book fell from a shelf above her, landing beside her. She looked up into the emptiness.

"Will nobody listen to me, ever?"

The book was a big dusty tome and she made an *oof* noise as she bent to pick it up. Then she closed her eyes, opened and pointed.

'Mortal'.

"OK, ghost," she said looking up. "So that's just freaky."

"Hey. Who are you talking to?" Carter leaned against a shelf watching her.

She slammed the book shut, raising a small cloud of dust.

"Nobody." She sneezed. "Passing time. You?"

He shrugged. "Bored."

"Me too."

She began sliding books back onto the shelves.

"Hungry?" he asked.

"God, yes."

"Want to go find some food?"

She held up her hand and Carter helped her up, then she strapped her weapon bag on with a martyred expression.

As they walked out from her hiding place she saw that many students were sprawled on the floor in various postures of rest. Rachel, playing cards with Alex at her First Aid table, waved perkily from across the room.

Jo was in a corner talking intently with Gabe.

Interesting.

Carter turned to see what she was looking at, then rolled his eyes.

"Catastrophic, you mean."

They found the dining room and headed on to the kitchen where a pot of sauce bubbled on the stove. Pasta drained in giant colanders in the sink.

"Spaghetti again," Allie said ruefully.

Carter lifted a towel on the counter to reveal a loaf of fresh bread. He sliced off two thick pieces which they slathered in butter and ate quickly before heading down the hall.

"So, are you ready?" Carter asked her as they walked aimlessly to the entrance hall and then back again.

"As I'll ever be, I guess." Allie said, licking butter off her fingertips. "I just want it to be over."

"Me too." His reply was so heartfelt that she glanced up at him, surprised.

"Do you think it's going to be bad?" she asked.

"Here's the thing," he said, stepping closer to her. "I don't want anything to happen to you. I kind of like having you around."

She smiled up at him. "You know what, Carter West? I kind of like having you around too."

He leaned down to hug her and she could feel his muscles through his shirt as he lifted her off the ground and swung her around until she giggled. He smiled broadly as he set her down, and she noticed that his eyes crinkled adorably. He looked like a different person when he really smiled, and she was aware that she had only rarely seen him look truly happy.

With no warning, he bent his head to kiss her delicately. Surprised, she breathed in his unique scent, feeling his cool breath in her mouth. She leaned into him, and when she wrapped her arms around his neck she felt his arms tighten on her waist.

She liked the way his mouth felt – soft but strong. And yet...

She had a flashing vision of the two of them fighting like Jo and Gabe. Not speaking for weeks because of jealousy and fear. Losing everything they already had.

This is such a bad idea.

Even though it was the last thing she wanted to do, she pulled away from him gently.

He looked dazed.

"I'm sorry," he said. "I just … I've wanted to do that for so long."

Me too.

For a moment, she leaned her head against his chest, feeling his arms around her. Because she could. Then she straightened. "Carter, I don't think..." She fumbled for the right words. "I don't know if this is right for us, right now. What if it messes everything up?"

The colour drained from his face. He put his hands in his pockets and looked at the floor.

Three breaths in and two out before he looked at her again.

When he did, his eyes were guarded. "It was just a kiss, Allie. We're not getting married."

She flushed at his tone, but tugged at his hand. "No, don't do that. I just need more time to think stuff through. Can you give me some time?"

Carter shrugged with studied carelessness. "Don't worry, it's fine. I shouldn't have done it. You're right. Now isn't the time. And the whole Sylvain thing only just happened. I understand."

He tried to pull away but she clung to him, wanting to say the thing that would make him meet her eyes again.

"Please, Carter. Don't be cross. I'm not saying no. I'm saying you're special to me – and what we have together is special. And I'm just confused. Can you wait? Wait for me to be sure?"

He looked up at her, his dark eyes wounded. "Allie, the only problem is, I don't know if you ever will be sure."

They walked back to the library in silence.

***

As darkness fell, the tension in the library was so thick Allie fancied she could see it hanging in the air like a fog.

By half past ten, most of the fighters were strapping on the armour she'd seen stacked up earlier in the day. They looked different in their gear. More grown-up. Dangerous.

Carter, who had been avoiding her all evening, looked like a proper soldier, dressed all in black with armour and weaponry strapped across his chest. He had knives in scabbards strapped to his right thigh and his left arm.

Even Rachel wore protective armour, and she pulled her black hair back into a long, flowing ponytail – a warrior princess.

She looked at Allie critically. "Just because you're not a fighter, they can't leave you with nothing. Come here."

Allie walked over obediently, and Rachel pulled a shield over her head, tightening the straps until it completely encased her torso.

Rachel held her at arm's length and nodded. "That's better."

If Allie thought the weapon bag was uncomfortable, being sheathed in armour was worse. Sitting down was virtually impossible as the shield dug into her thighs. She leaned against a table, uncomfortably.

"Great," she muttered. "I might live, but do I want to?"

Without looking up at her Rachel scoffed, "Yes. Next question?"

The feeling of chaos that had permeated all elements of the school for the last few days was long gone, replaced by brutal order. The students were silent and mechanical as they prepared. Instead of barking orders, the teachers spoke quietly.

By eleven o'clock, the frontline fighters were ready to move out. Watching Gabe and Sylvain prepare to leave, Allie felt a wave of melancholy. They looked so strong and determined, yet she knew they must be frightened. When Sylvain smiled at her seductively while strapping a long knife to his thigh, she surprised herself by smiling back.

He could die out there. No grudges in trenches.

She looked over at Jo, who stood nearby watching Gabe prepare. She looked bereft.

Once they were ready, the frontline fighters gathered together in a circle, their armour and weaponry jangling in the suddenly silent library. Their faces were resolute and betrayed no doubt. Zelazny stood among them, talking in a voice so low that Allie couldn't hear his words. After a moment, they walked out of the room, single file, without a backward glance.

The library was quiet after they left, but already the second-line fighters were preparing to go too. Allie, Jo and Rachel stood together watching as Lucas and Jules checked each other's armour.

"No way," Rachel whispered, looking to her left.

Allie followed her eyes to see that the team had been joined by a new fighter – Lisa. Clad all in black, and in body armour that seemed to have been moulded just for her slim figure, she gripped a knife in her teeth as she checked the strength of the ties holding a scabbard on her upper arm.

She didn't look up at them as she walked out of the building with the others.

Carter was to monitor the battle by listening to everyone's thoughts, so he set himself up on top of the librarian's tall desk.

Allie walked over and tugged on his foot.

"Hey, good luck," she said. "We're counting on you."

He smiled at her, but his eyes looked distant. "Thanks, Allie. Same to you."

The minutes ticked by with agonising slowness. Rachel straightened her bandages for the thousandth time, while Allie paced the floor, her arms wrapped around her shielded torso. She felt sick with anticipation, her stomach churning from nerves. What if it went wrong? What if people died?

What if they lost?

Eloise stood near Carter in a state of such unnatural stillness that Allie wondered if she was breathing. Jo huddled miserably in a chair, staring at the floor.

Suddenly Carter's voice split the silence. "It's begun."

"Too early," Eloise whispered, staring at him. "Trap."

Allie looked at her watch. It was half past eleven.

Eloise pulled herself together, clouds clearing from her expression. "Where are they?" she asked briskly.

"Near the summerhouse," he replied, his voice oddly devoid of emotion. "The second line were ambushed. The first line are backtracking to help them."

"OK!" Eloise leapt to her feet and motioned to the others. "Something's not right. Get ready. Nobody leaves this room. Jo, bar the door."

Jo stumbled out of her lethargy and ran to the entrance, pulling a heavy metal bar down and locking it into place.

"Allie, stay with me," Eloise said. "I want you by my side constantly."

Too numb with fear to ask questions, Allie moved closer to her.

"Tom, Alex and Bill, check the perimeter of this room. If you hear or sense any sign of intrusion into any part of the building let me know immediately."

The three disappeared into the stacks of books.

Allie matched Eloise's stride as she paced, sticking to her side like a limpet.

Carter gave frequent updates in a strange, mechanical cadence.

"They've pushed the second-line back into the woods."

"The first-line has arrived to assist the second."

"The fighting is intense."

"Lucas is wounded but it's not severe. He's being brought in."

"Anna is wounded."

"Lisa is wounded but refusing aid."

Allie and Jo exchanged a look. Allie's chest felt tight. This was what she'd been afraid of, and it was all happening.

She concentrated so closely on his updates and Eloise's responses that when she felt the tell-tale tingling sensation at first she just scratched her head absently. Then she froze. It was Nathaniel, trying to reach her mind. She knew that feeling — like a needle in her skull.

She looked at Carter, calling out to him soundlessly. *He's in my head.*

His eyes met hers across the room. He knew what this meant. If she shut the door in her mind to Nathaniel, then the two of them couldn't talk to each other, either. They would each be alone in this. Solemnly, he nodded his understanding. It was the only way.

She shut the door. He held her gaze for a second and then looked away.

"Someone is attempting to command Allie," he reported calmly.

Eloise spun around and grabbed her arm. "Are you OK?" she asked, her face taut.

"I'm fine," Allie told her, although she wasn't. She was too scared to be fine. "I've blocked it."

"They're close, then," Eloise said, her lips a thin line. "They've got past them." She turned around. "Carter, let August know that—"

A loud crash outside the library cut her off.

Everyone looked at the solid oak doors as Eloise finished the thought. "… they're in the building."

At the sound of running footsteps, Allie turned to see Alex and the other two fighters hurtling towards them from the back of the room. The students formed a line inside the door, gripping their swords in their hands.

"Allie, I want you behind us," Eloise barked.

I can't believe this is happening, Allie thought.

She looked around the room, taking in the battle line by the door. Carter standing tall atop the librarian's desk, scanning the room as he gave quiet updates to Eloise who stood nearby, holding a knife in a clenched fist.

And to think, all I did was spray-paint a door, Allie thought.

She sensed a movement behind her and turned to see Jo drifting across the room towards her. Her smile was wide and out of place. The way she was walking – almost floating – was all wrong. Allie watched cautiously as she approached.

Jo opened her mouth but the voice that came out was deep, baritone. Male.

"Alyson Sheridan. At last. I need to talk to you. I'm sorry you're blocking me. Open yourself to me so that I can explain."

It was Nathaniel's voice. Allie felt her chest squeeze around her heart. Her throat was so constricted she feared she might not be able to speak. The others were all focused on the door and hadn't yet noticed what was happening.

"I don't need your explanations," she said breathlessly. "Let Jo go. Do not use my friends as your mouthpieces."

Her words alerted Eloise, and she wheeled around with her stake raised.

Jo gave her an irritated look and shoved her mildly. The force sent her flying across the room into a wall of books. She slid to the floor, limp. Allie bit back a scream.

"Don't make me hurt anybody else," the man's voice said from Jo's mouth as Allie struggled to breathe. "Open yourself and let me in."

"No," she said, gasping for air. "If you want to talk to me then you come to this school yourself. I don't talk to cowards who use teenage girls to shield themselves."

The room was going black around the edges. As she fell to her knees she saw Jo collapse. Carter leapt off the table and was at her side in an instant. She could hear someone shouting as everything blurred.

The next thing she knew, Carter was carrying her in his arms.

"She's hyperventilating," he said, laying her gently on the floor near Rachel's table.

Rachel knelt beside her as Carter ran back across the room. "Breathe slowly and evenly," she said calmly.

Allie forced air into her lungs. "Jo…" she gasped.

"She's fine," Rachel promised. "She's resting."

Strands of air filled Allie's lungs and the darkness receded. Just as her head began to clear, though, A huge crash split the quiet. The library doors bowed from the force of an unseen blow but held.

All the fighters stood ready. Carter was back at his spot on the desk. There was no more time to recover.

Rachel stood up, pulling Allie to her feet. "Get ready," she warned, her voice grim.

A second crash split the mighty bar in two, and the doors burst open. A stream of fighters in glittering armour shot through the door.

Then the lights went out.

In the sudden darkness, Allie was disoriented. She could hear the clashing metal of fighting across the room but she could see nothing at all. She took a step forward and stumbled over something soft and heavy.

Reaching down, she realised it was Jo – still unconscious at her feet. She couldn't leave her there — it wasn't safe.

She put her hands under Jo's arms and dragged her until she lay underneath Rachel's table. Then she began to feel her way cautiously towards where she thought the fighting must be. But it was easy to get confused in such a large space in the dark, and soon she didn't know where she was.

She stopped for a moment to listen – the fighting was still quite far away. But she had to at least see what was going on. Maybe she could help.

Reaching out in front of her, she found only air. Hesitantly, she took a step to the right, but as she did she thought she heard a faint voice whisper, "No."

The voice was rough and hoarse – as if it wasn't used often. She stood still, peering into the gloom, but could see nothing at all. She took a tentative step to the left. This time the voice was clearer. "Yes".

Another step to the left, another whispered affirmation. She followed the whispered directions until the voice, which now seemed to be fading, said, "Stop".

The noise around her indicated that she was closer to the fighting. She could hear the clanging of metal against metal, and the shouts of the victorious and the wounded ringing out above a low rumbling noise that sounded like growling.

Reaching out to either side, she could tell she was between two tall bookcases.

"Why here?" she whispered.

The voice was so faint now that she could barely make it out in the general cacophony. She could have sworn it said, "Safer here."

She stared in the direction of the battle sounds but could only barely make out shapes moving rapidly in the darkness. If she was to have any idea what was going on, she knew there was only one way.

Cautiously, she opened the door.

Carter? Can you hear me?

There was no reply, but through their connection she was overwhelmed with nightmarish impressions of a violent battle – brief glimpses of swords rising and plunging, contorted expressions and guttural screams.

It was too much to take. She covered her face with her arms.

When she lifted her head again seconds later, the room was suffused with a faint green glow. She could just make out Rachel darting across the room, her jaw set determinedly, breaking glow sticks to turn them on and then throwing them on the floor to spread light.

Now she could make out the hazy silhouette of the fighters across the room. She saw that Eloise was back on her feet, wielding a sword so expertly that to Allie it was just a flash of light. To her right, Sylvain was using the skills he'd tried to teach them earlier – a dagger in each hand, he moved through the crowd with brutal confidence.

But their opponents outnumbered them. They were an impressive opponent, in glittering silver armour, like the angels in the library paintings. They moved with unbelievable speed and grace. And they, too, were young and beautiful.

Even with no experience in battle, Allie could see that the Cimmeria fighters, intimidating in their black armour, worked together elegantly. They threw each other weapons, caught them smoothly, leapt balletically to back each other up.

But what they weren't doing was winning.

They were being pushed back into the library, slowly but steadily. Before long they'd be fighting with their backs to the wall.

And Carter – where was Carter?

She searched each face in the pale glow until she saw him at the heart of the battle. His opponent was a tenacious fighter, but they seemed evenly skilled. The fighter was tall and slim, with dark blond hair. She noticed that they each used brute force with little finesse, so the fighter must be new to this as well. And there was something familiar about him. She leaned forward and peered into the faint light cast by a dying glow-stick at their feet, trying to make out his features.

Suddenly she gasped and jumped backward, nearly falling as she tripped over a book. She felt her chest squeeze again and fought to keep her breathing even.

It couldn't be him. It's dark. She struggled to calm herself. *It can't Christopher.*

"*It is.*" The voice in her head was not Carter's.

What do you want from me? In her head she was screaming.

Nathanael's voice was calm and soothing. "*I want to talk to you.*"

A tear escaped and ran down her cheek.

Why? Why are you doing this?

He had a deep, hollow laugh.

"*Oh, this isn't all about you, Alyson. Don't worry. But you are part of it. You are special, as you are no doubt beginning to realise. And I would just like the chance to talk to you.*"

Allie felt the panic in her chest morph into righteous indignation. She took a deep angry breath.

I already told you, that if you want to talk to me, you'll have to do it in person.

"*If I do that, all of your friends will die. I presume that is not what you want?*"

Allie watched Eloise send one silver-clad fighter flying into the door and without hesitation turn to engage another.

No.

"*Then here are my terms. You agree to come and join me, and I will make all this stop now. I will withdraw my fighters, and Cimmeria can continue as it was.*"

Allie glared into the darkness. *I thought you said this wasn't about me.*

"*I spoke the truth,*" he said. "*Isabelle is teaching a twisted view of who we are. Our young are being ruined by her. Misled. Lied to. I've asked her to stop and she has refused. Teaching us to live like bovine humans is unnatural. She's perverting our race. She is a threat to our very nature. With me, you will learn the reality of who we are. You will join us. Help us. Be one of us.*"

Allie considered this.

So, if I join you, you'll bide your time and when you're good and ready you'll attack again. Only this time I'll be on your side and somehow this will help you?

There was a pause before he replied. "*It is what has to be.*"

I don't think so. I will never join you. You will have to kill me to take me with you, and what good would that do? I am a Cimmerian now. She took a step forwards as if he were standing in front of her. *And you know what? My mother told me never to talk to strangers.*

With that, she closed the door in her mind.

Reaching into her weapon bag, she pulled out one of the metal-tipped stakes that Sylvain had given her and hefted it, feeling its weight. It seemed to vibrate in her hands as if it had a power of its own, and longed to be used.

But as she stepped out of her hiding place, a rush of air blew her hair back and a powerful hand grabbed her by the shoulder. She swung around, flailing her stake, but a dismissive blow from her attacker sent it flying.

She looked into a pair of puzzled green eyes.

She was only a girl, younger than Allie, maybe thirteen years old. She was small, with light brown hair tied back in a bouncy ponytail. But she wore the gleaming silver armour of Nathanael's army and she held a very large knife in her right hand.

"Hang on," she said, wrinkling her noise slightly. "Are you ... human?"

Allie stared, astonished. The girl seemed so normal. She could easily be a Cimmeria student.

"Yes," she admitted, finally.

The girl studied her for a minute, her head cocked to one side, then shrugged.

"Sucks to be you," she said perkily, raising her knife and swinging it so quickly that Allie didn't have time to react.

But the blade never touched her. A dark hand gripped the girl's wrist, twisting it brutally.

"I don't think so, *cherie*." Sylvain said. Then, with an awful sound like a twig snapping, he broke her arm.

She screamed and dropped the knife.

Sylvain raised his sword to finish her off, and Allie grabbed his arm. "Sylvain, no!"

He looked surprised as she held onto his wrist, her eyes pleading. "She's only a girl."

When she looked back, though, the girl had disappeared.

Sylvain shook his head, but his voice was sympathetic. "They are all only girls and boys, Allie. And she would have killed you."

She knew he was right, but she wasn't sorry. "Thank you for saving me."

He smiled, and his white teeth gleamed in the dark room. "Any time, *ma puce*. But one thing…" He wrapped his arm around her waist, there was a rush of air, and suddenly they were deep in the library.

Allie stared around her, lost. The fighting sounded far away. She could barely see Sylvain in the dark.

"I suggest you stay back here," he said. "Away from danger."

And then he was gone.

For a second she stood motionless, trying to get her bearings. It had all happened so quickly.

A book tumbling off the top shelf startled her from her reverie. Another one, flew right at her. Instinctively, she caught it, and looked up just as another flew off, landing on the rolling library ladder beside her.

The ladder gave her an idea.

It led up to the highest shelves. The bookcase was about twelve feet tall and solid. She climbed the ladder tentatively, and discovered that it ended just shy of the top. With a little effort, she pulled herself the rest of the way up. There was plenty of room for her to perch on top of the bookcase. From there, she could see out over the library where the fighting continued.

The Cimmeria team had been pushed even further into the room, and the battle now ranged all over the library. She could see Jerry and Eloise fighting back-to-back against three opponents. Carter and Gabe were using a similar tactic on the other side of the room.

But despite their bravery and skill, Allie could see that they were surrounded. There was no way they could win.

They were better fighters than their opponents, but they were outnumbered. It was just a matter of time.

She felt a sickening lurch of fear in the pit of her stomach. What would Nathanael do to them? Would he kill them all? And what about her? Would she stay hiding here until it was all over, and then be captured by Nathanael and used as another one of his weapons?

She pulled a knife from her weapon bag and hefted it. It felt strangely warm, as if it were alive. She remembered how easily the girl had swatted her weapon away, as if she'd been holding a pen rather than a stake that could cut through meat like butter. She would be killed or taken almost immediately. She couldn't help at all.

Tears of frustration prickled at the backs of her eyes, and she forced herself to watch the fight. If they were going to lose, she was going be there when it happened. She would see it all.

But as she watched the fighters moving in their dangerous dance, she noticed something odd by the door. She leaned forwards for a better look, rubbing her eyes roughly with the backs of her hands.

It was a blur, that then disappeared. After a moment, there was another one.

She slid over to the very edge of the bookcase to try and see more clearly.

For a long moment there was nothing and she thought she might have imagined it. Then... Yes! There it was again. It was a kind of haze and then it stopped.

And became a man, in black armour with a sword.

Then, another one.

And a woman, a knife in her hand, crouching low to the ground.

They were fighters, moving so fast that she saw them as a blur. Only when they stopped could she see them.

Within moments, there were twice as many Cimmeria fighters as opponents. The new fighters were very fast, and very good. One in particular dispatched his opponents with such speed that she found it hard to take her eyes off him. He was extraordinary, leaping gracefully from one fight to the next. He used a knife rather than a sword.

He was devastating.

It was glorious to watch. Allie's heart leapt. Whoever these fighters were, they were changing everything.

Nathanael's crew did not give in easily, and Allie could not help but admire their tenacity. But the outcome was clear already, and in minutes, it was over. The invaders melted away. She never saw them leave – one minute they were there.

The next they weren't.

Chapter Twenty-one

The end count was not, as bad as they'd expected. Seven were wounded – three quite severely, including Zelazny, whose blood-drained body had been carried in by sombre students.

Gabe thought the numbers had been about the same among Nathanael's troops. She heard him tell Isabelle, "I don't think anyone was killed. But some were immobilised by their injuries."

"So we ended up even." She sounded weary.

Jo was awake but pale, and said she had a pounding headache. She thought she'd been hit on the head in the fray. Nobody had the heart to tell her the truth.

As soon as Rachel didn't need her anymore, Allie went looking for Carter. She found him unstrapping his armour and throwing it into the pile in a corner of the library.

"You OK?" she asked.

"Yeah. You?"

"I'm good." She stuck her hands in her pockets. "Did you hear about Zelazny?"

Carter nodded, looking worried. "Is there any word...?"

She shook her head. "We're waiting."

Carter ran his hands through his dark hair. He seemed exhausted.

"During the fight he talked to me."

He looked at her sharply. "Who, Nathanael?"

"Yes."

"What did he want?"

"He asked me to join him. He said he'd stop all this if I would."

Carter threw his knife onto a pile with such force that it bounced up again, before coming to rest.

"I don't understand it. Why the hell is he obsessed with you?" She could hear frustration in his voice.

"I wish I knew."

She stood still, watching him organise the weapons, his face troubled. Then she made up her mind.

"And Carter? That blond guy you were fighting?" Their eyes met. "That was my brother."

***

"Are you certain, Allie?" Isabelle's golden brown eyes watched her closely.

It was late afternoon the day after the battle, and Allie and Carter were in Isabelle's office, along with Eloise and Matthew. Having slept fitfully for a few hours and then spent the day helping to clean the library, she'd finally decided to tell the school's leaders what she believed she'd seen the night before.

Isabelle was sitting behind her desk with Matthew standing at her shoulder. Allie and Carter sat in the soft chairs across from her. Eloise leaned with her back against the door and her arms crossed. She looked worried.

"It was dark and chaotic. It would be easy to make a mistake," Isabelle said gently.

Allie was adamant. "My brother was my best friend. I would know him anywhere."

Carter moved the conversation on. "If it was her brother, though, what does that mean? It could explain Nathanael's obsession with Allie."

"It could mean any number of things," Isabelle replied thoughtfully. "It could mean that he knows her brother has certain skills that Allie is also

149

likely to have. Or it could mean something completely different. We just don't..."

"Don't you think it's time," Carter interrupted her brusquely, "that we all understood just why Allie is here? What is it about her? Why is she so important?"

The room fell silent. At last, somebody had asked the question – the one she herself had never been brave enough to ask, in part because she wasn't sure she wanted to know the answer.

Isabelle's expression did not change, although Allie could sense that she was deciding how to proceed. But in the end it was Matthew who spoke.

"Allie has a unique bloodline."

She didn't like his choice of words. It made her sound like a racehorse.

"She's too young yet for us to know if she received the right set of genes to become the kind of woman her grandmother was, but if she did..."

He paused as if deciding how much to reveal. "If she did she could be powerful."

Stunned, Allie stared at him silently.

"Powerful in what way?" Carter asked the question she was too stunned to form.

Matthew and Isabelle exchanged a long look that seemed to convey volumes. This time, Isabelle replied.

"Allie's grandmother and great-grandmother were witches," she said.

Allie searched her face for any indication that this was some sort of joke. But she was deadly serious.

She turned to Carter, but his expression was as baffled as her own. "She's a *witch*?" His voice rose incredulously.

"She could be," Matthew corrected him. "We don't know yet."

Allie felt a mix of excitement and fear. Not immortal then. Something else.

Carter and Eloise both looked as if they couldn't believe what they were hearing.

"Are there witches?" Eloise asked, in a tone of disbelief. "I find it hard to believe that such entities exists, Isabelle."

"Almost none do," the headmistress said, simply. "That's why she's here. I believe, as Nathanael believes, that her grand-mother and great-grandmother were witches, posing as humans. But we have no proof. Even if it was true, there's no way to know if Allie inherited their abilities." Her words trailed off.

"Is that why Christopher disappeared?" Allie hadn't meant to speak aloud. Her own voice startled her.

Isabelle looked at her. "We don't know. Until today, we weren't even certain that Nathanael had him. But we feared he might."

Allie nodded, although her thoughts were troubled. Could Christopher have run away to join Nathanael? Was he a witch? Was he trying to reach her or was he being used as a lure?

"This is a lot for us to absorb, Isabelle." Eloise sounded dubious. "I have always been taught – and believed – that witches were as mythical as trolls or…" she searched for the right word "…pixies."

Matthew turned to her. "We do understand that, Eloise. Until Allie started manifesting some abilities recently, we expected nothing to come of this. We were just being careful after Christopher disappeared in case there was something to it. Now… Well, frankly, now we're beginning to wonder."

His rich voice reminded Allie uncomfortably of Nathanael's, and she studied him curiously. Who was he? Why did nobody know anything about him?

"Would she be like Mr Ellison?" Carter asked.

Matthew turned his intense eyes on Carter.

"Mr Ellison has knowledge and skills associated with mystical ceremonies once well-known and practiced among our people, but which have been largely lost over the years. His family passed them down through the generations," he explained. "He's a seer and a protector. But he's not a witch."

They were all looking at Allie, as if she they might see the power on her skin. Flushing, she said, "I don't understand anything."

Isabelle stood. "This is new to all of us, Allie, in many ways. We are all trying to figure out what is real and what isn't, and what Nathanael is really up to. Give it time. It's entirely possible that you're a particularly sensitive and gifted human, and that you and Carter simply have a unique connection to one another and nothing more. So, please, don't feel that you are under any pressure to do or to be anything. We could be on the wrong track entirely with this. Only time will tell."

Eloise dismissed the entire witch conversation with a flick of her long hair. "Speaking of Nathanael," she said the name with contempt, "have we heard anything from him?"

Isabelle shook her head. "Nothing so far. I've sent messages, but there has been no reply."

"What happens if this isn't resolved before autumn term begins?" Carter asked.

Isabelle held out her hands helplessly. "We will have to decide whether to go forward with it. My feeling is that Nathanael would like nothing more than for us to cancel, and that is almost in itself reason enough to proceed. There will be a Council meeting tonight, and we will decide then what to do. But my instincts say we should not give into him. He must see that we won't back down."

Allie listened quietly, hoping they'd reveal more insight about how Cimmeria really worked.

As if she'd heard her thoughts, Isabelle turned to her. "Could you excuse us, Allie? We need to talk privately about a few things."

Allie bristled. If she was a witch, she should be part of things, shouldn't she? But Isabelle's expression told her that arguing would be futile. With a sigh, she walked out, the door closing quietly behind her. s

Back in the library, things were gradually getting back to normal. The room remained the main hub of activity. Weapons had been removed, blood scrubbed from the floor. Tables were arranged strategically, covered with papers and tea cups. Rachel was curled up in a leather chair talking quietly with Jo.

"Hey, how are you?" Allie asked.

Jo was still pale, but largely recovered.

"I'm OK, but I can't remember anything." She glanced around at her friends. " Seriously, tell me. Does anybody know what happened to me?"

Allie and Rachel exchanged a look. Then, Allie sat down on the floor in front of Jo and told her what Nathanael had done. As she stopped speaking, Jo shuddered.

"I feel sick."

Rachel bent over to place an arm around her friend, and gave her a hug. "Nathanael's a complete tosser."

Allie stretched out her legs. "So, the guys who came to help? They were the Council?"

Rachel nodded. "Aren't they awesome?"

"Was your dad there?" Allie asked.

"Oh, yes," Rachel rolled her eyes. "Right in the middle of everything, as usual. I haven't had a chance to talk to him yet, but he waved at me."

"I wonder why they didn't come sooner?"

Leaning forwards confidentially, Jo whispered. "Gabe said Isabelle wanted to handle Nathanael on her own. She thought it would make things worse if she got in a big army of defenders. But after last night she decided... Well, you know, screw it. Better to take the risk of aggravating Nathanael then lose Cimmeria altogether. So, she got in touch with everybody and asked them to come as quickly as possible."

Allie was dying to tell them about what had just happened in Isabelle's office, but she stopped herself. What if it changed the way they looked at her?

Right now, she was still one of them. She liked the feeling of being part of something. For the first time in her life she fit in somewhere, and she wanted that to last.

And so, in the end, she said nothing.

But she knew someday they would learn the truth. And that would be the end of everything.

Chapter Twenty-two

The sound of raucous voices and slamming doors woke Allie with a start. She checked the clock by her bed – 3.30 a.m.

She grabbed her dressing gown and headed out of the room. The robe fluttered behind her like a bride's train as she hurried down the first flight of stairs.

Jo and Lisa stood in the dark on the landing – Jo looking like a blonde fairy in her pink satin dressing gown, and Lisa was nearly invisible in black jeans and black top.

"What's happening?" Allie whispered.

"The Council is gathering," Jo whispered back. "Everybody who wasn't here last night is arriving."

"Not that we need them." Lisa made no attempt to lower her voice.

Allie and Jo exchanged a look and then turned to look over the banister. They could make out shapes moving in the dark, and hear snippets of conversation.

"I wonder who…" Allie began, then she stifled a scream as a heavy hand fell on her shoulder.

"Spying, are we?"

The Yorkshire accent came from a very tall man – at least, Allie thought, six-foot-five – with dark skin, sharply defined features and strangely familiar almond-shaped eyes. She felt she'd seen him somewhere before. Then it hit her. He was the amzing fighter from last night. The one who had turned the battle in Cimmeria's favour.

He had a hand on Jo's shoulder too. Lisa had disappeared.

"We just…" Allie looked to Jo for help but she stood silent, staring at him, terrified.

"Dad. Quit teasing them." Rachel's voice came from the landing above them, and the man turned and bounded up the stairs so quickly Allie wasn't certain she'd actually seen him do it.

He wrapped his daughter in a bear hug. "How's my girl?"

Rachel looked embarrassed but smiled despite herself.

"I'm fine, Dad. Have you saved the day again?"

"Of course! When Cimmeria calls, I'm there. Do you want to hear me sing the school song?"

"Cimmeria doesn't have a school song, Dad. And, no. Nobody here wants to hear you sing."

Jo and Allie listened to the conversation from the foot of the stairs, occasionally exchanging astonished looks.

"Are you going to introduce me to your friends? I really should apologise to them, I came up looking for you, but when I saw them spying I couldn't resist."

Allie and Jo walked down the stairs together, and Rachel waved awkwardly.

"Guys, this is my dad. Dad, these are my friends Allie and Jo."

He held out his hand to each of them in turn. "John Patel. It's my pleasure to meet you both. And I apologise for startling you earlier. As Rachel will no doubt explain, my sense of humour is unacceptable."

They each mumbled polite greetings, stealing glances at Rachel, who looked mortified.

"When's the Council meeting?" she asked to change the subject.

"The first meeting starts shortly – most people are here now. But I wanted to say hello before then." He looked at his watch regretfully. "I should probably go now, sweetheart. I'll come and find you when we get out."

He kissed her lightly on the cheek and then disappeared down the stairs in an instant.

For a moment, they stood quietly. Then they all began at once.

"Scared us to death…"

"Your dad's kind of cool…"

"Really sorry, you guys…"

Allie had to smile. "He seems really happy to see you."

"Yeah, I know," Rachel conceded with a reluctant smile. "I'm such an ungrateful child."

They sat in a row on the top stair, listening to the activity below them.

"What's this Council thing all about?" Allie asked, after a while.

"It's like the government for those of us who think Isabelle's right about how we should all live," Rachel explained. "You know. Peaceful, no killing, big love … that sort of thing."

Allie and Jo nodded.

"Anyway," she continued, "they usually meet once a year after the winter ball, and it's like a big party. But they can be summoned at any time if it all goes tits up. And, in case you haven't noticed, it's all gone tits up."

"So they're deciding what to do next?" Jo asked.

"Basically. I guess they'll discuss Nathanael, and then they'll send a messenger, and then he'll send one back, and blah, blah, blah." She waved a dismissive hand. "Now that they're all here, I don't think he'll bother us anymore. He really will not want to mess with the Council. As you saw last night, they're hardcore."

They sat on the stairs for twenty minutes or so, listening to snippets of conversation and the sounds of people moving around the ground floor. The bustle of activity was nice after the unnatural hush in the school for the last week.

After a while, though, Allie yawned hugely. "Sorry, guys. I'd love to stay up all night and see if anything else happens but I'm wiped out."

Jo stood up with her and stretched. "Me too. Will you be OK, Rachel?"

Rachel nodded vigorously, her ponytail bouncing. "I'll be fine. I'm going to wait for my dad. I'll see you two in the morning."

Jo and Allie trooped back up to the dormitory floor.

"Hey," Allie said, "What's up with you and Gabe now? Are you back together?"

Jo made a face. "We're talking, but we're not together. Lucas and I broke up, though. He's been very cool about everything. I think he knows

I kind of went crazy for a while. He doesn't seem angry about it. I need just some time. Eloise made me promise to be single for a while, and I'm trying to."

They hugged in the hallway and then Jo went on to her room. Twenty minutes later, in her own bed, tired, but unable to sleep, Allie lay thinking about what had happened in Isabelle's office. If she actually did have special powers, she could help them save the school. And yet, all she seemed to be able to offer at the moment was the ability to get in the way, hyperventilate at the first sign of stress, and pass out.

"They're lucky to have me," she mumbled as she curled up to sleep.

***

The next morning at breakfast the Council was the main subject of conversation. Any unknown adults spotted in the halls were instantly presumed to be Council members. Most of the alumni kept a low profile, but a few sat together at one table talking discreetly.

"I heard they're going to make a deal with him," Allie heard Jules whisper loudly to Lucas at the next table. "Something to make him go away."

"What could they give him?" he asked.

She cast a meaningful look at Allie, who quickly averted her eyes, her stomach flipping.

"That's ridiculous, Jules," Lucas responded. "There's no way they'd do that."

"Well, they won't sacrifice all of us for one person, surely?"

"She's not all he wants," Lucas said, angrily.

When Rachel appeared toting a tray with toast and cereal, Allie was relieved. It struck her that, at some point over the last week or two, she'd come to rely on Rachel more than almost anybody. Except Carter.

"Hey, sit," she commanded. "Be with me. Save me from the evil gossip of Jules."

Rachel gave her a quizzical look. "What's she bitchi... I mean gossiping about now?"

"Me. Unfortunately."

"Oh, for God's sake."

Rachel settled in next to her and buttered her toast thickly, before biting into it with a happy sigh.

"I love toast, Allie, I'm not going to lie to you."

"I know you do, babe. Your love for toast is pure and beautiful."

Rachel took another bite and smiled dreamily. "Don't judge me, world."

Allie giggled and sipped her apple juice. "How'd things go last night with your dad?"

Rachel nodded. "Fine. He was on his best behaviour. Bringing presents, promising to be chilled. It was good."

Allie spoke cautiously. "I liked him, you know? He seemed kind of fun. Like one of us."

Rachel chewed reflectively. "Yeah, I can see that. I think it's almost always easier to like other people's parents than it is to like your own. Your own family is always the one that drives you crazy. I'd probably really like your parents."

"No, you wouldn't," Allie said, without missing a beat.

Rachel chuckled and reached for the jam.

They ate in companionable silence for a while, then Rachel set her knife down. "Oh my God, I can't believe I almost forgot to tell you." Lowering her voice to a whisper, she said, "Dad told me the Council has given Nathanael an ultimatum about you. I don't know all the details, but I think it's along the lines of 'No way, you wanker. Dad brought the message to him personally last night, so they didn't waste any time."

Allie felt oddly thrilled to know that Rachel's father was representing her – protecting her.

"What did Nathanael say?" she asked.

"Dad said he was ... how did he put it? 'Defiant but not stupid'."

With her knife, Allie drew a question mark in the butter on her plate. When she spoke, her voice was unnaturally calm.

"What do you think that means?"

"I think it means that Nathanael was like 'you are not the boss of me… But, actually, is that the time? Maybe I'll just go.'"

Allie exhaled slowly. Maybe it was over at last. With an army of Cimmeria supporters, including some sort of Superman in the form of Rachel's dad, the school was very well protected.

Rachel was still talking. "Dad thinks that's it for him now. He says he'll probably come back at some point, but maybe not for a long time. Oh, and Isabelle's asked Dad to stick around for a while to make sure. He's agreed. He spends a lot of the year in Asia these days, and he doesn't want to be so far away. Just in case."

Allie brightened. "That really makes me feel better, Rachel. I mean, I know you like your independence, but after the last couple of months, it will be great to have somebody like your dad here."

Rachel shrugged. "Don't worry about me. I'll deal with it. Maybe if he's around we'll get over some of our 'issues'. Who knows? Stranger things have happened. Lately. Here."

***

Allie hadn't seen Carter since the meeting in Isabelle's office. But that evening in the common room, he was the first person she saw. He was sitting in the same leather chair he'd sat in the first time she'd ever walked into that room with a book on his lap, watching her.

"Hey," she said, perching lightly on a leather ottoman.

"Hey back." His voice was studiedly normal.

"Haven't seen you in a couple of days. How's it been with the alums?" She pretended to be normal too, but her hands betrayed her, winding the hem of her shirt around her fingers.

"Good. Busy, but good. How are you dealing with everything?" He set his book down on the floor; she couldn't quite make out the title in the shadow of his chair.

"I'm a bit freaked out, but I'm dealing. I'm still thinking everything through." She looked at him earnestly. "What could it all mean, Carter?

Why is my brother fighting for him? And how could my grandmother – or I – be a … a you-know-what? You don't really believe they exist, do you?"

He studied her for a moment. "To be honest, Allie, I don't know what to think anymore. If you are, then you are, and what I was taught was wrong, then that's fine. Actually, it's kind of amazing. I mean, imagine being the only one of something. You really could be the only one in the whole world. That would make you kind of god-like. And even if you're not, you have this incredible heritage."

She could see that he was right, but it was still bittersweet. To be the only one of anything felt lonely. Forever an outsider. Her lip trembled.

"The only thing is, I was just getting used to the idea of maybe being one of you. And now. I'm not."

He reached out and took her hand, holding it gently in his – she felt a surge of energy flow into her. He turned it over so her palm faced up. With the most delicate of touches, he traced the shallow lines that crisscrossed it.

The lifeline. The heart line.

Her whole body tingled, and she shivered lightly.

"Whatever happens, Allie, whatever you are or are not, you are one of us now. Family is more than blood, I know better than most."

He looked at her with such naked longing that she held her breath. His eyes were deep, dark pools. She couldn't tear her gaze away. She had worked so hard not to feel drawn to him. Not to let things between them get confused.

But now things were confused.

She reached up to touch his face, tracing the strong line of his jaw to the tip of his chin.

"I would be honoured to be part of your family," she whispered.

He held her hands to his lips and kissed her fingertips. Heat rushed through her entire body. His eyes never left hers, and she could imagine kissing him – properly this time. Her cheeks flushed. She didn't know which one of them had summoned the image. She didn't really care. He pulled her closer and she tilted her head, knowing that if he kissed her now it would change everything between them forever.

"Well, isn't this a cosy scene."

Carter's shoulders fell. "Oh, do mind your own business, Sylvain," he snapped.

Allie let go of Carter's hands, but didn't turn around.

"I just wanted to say hello to Allie, and to allow her to thank me again for saving her life," Sylvain's voice was smug.

Carter gave Allie a surprised look. "What is he talking about?"

He didn't know. She hadn't had a chance to tell him what had happened during the battle, and he must have been too busy fighting to sense her fear at the time.

"It's true," she conceded, feeling oddly guilty. "A girl with a knife … during the battle. It was close, Carter. Sylvain appeared just when…"

Carter's eyes darkened. He stood up. "Well, how handy for you, Sylvain. Always there to save the day."

Sylvain smiled modestly. "I do the best I can."

Frowning, Carter turned back to Allie. "Let's go somewhere more private. Somewhere we can talk."

She started to nod, but Sylvain interrupted smoothly, "So sorry to disappoint, but August has asked for you, Carter. Can you come immediately?"

Zelazny had recovered, and was now coordinating Night School activities from his classroom, working with John Patel and other members of the Council. Sylvain looked distinctly not sorry, Allie thought.

Carter gave her a wistful look. "I have to…"

Allie nodded, keeping the disappointment off her face. She heard Carter mutter "cock" as he passed Sylvain on his way to the door.

Sylvain laughed. "Charming." When Carter was gone, he stepped closer to Allie and his face became more serious. "I did, really, want to make sure that you were fine. Are you fine? What happened was frightening. If I had not got to you in time…"

Allie wanted still to be angry at Sylvain. What he'd done was unforgiveable. But he'd saved her life more than once. The whole thing left her confused and lost. How was she supposed to feel?

"Thank you, Sylvain, for being there," she said, her tone formal. "You really did save me."

He smiled, as if he knew what she was thinking. "And do you forgive me yet, pretty Allie, for being such a *bête noir*? It was only because I wanted you so much. Because I found you irresistible."

Her face hardened. She wasn't about to grant him absolution. "Are you ever going to do that again to anybody? Ever?"

He shook his head with a fervency she didn't trust.

"Fine. If you never do that again to any girl in your whole immortal life, then I will forgive you."

He looked delighted. "My whole life may be very long, Allie," he teased.

"I don't care," she shot back. "You are only forgiven if you never do it again."

"Then the impossible has happened," he said. "Allie Sheridan has forgiven me and will be my friend."

"I didn't say I'd be your friend." She glared.

His blue eyes studied hers. "You will, though."

"Don't get your hopes up, Sylvain," she said, turning to the door. "Some things really are impossible."

She could hear him laughing as she walked down the hall.

Strange as Angels

And finally. This is the last scrap of unpublished Night School from the deep, dark past. In fact, it was tucked away for so long, I wasn't sure I still had it until I stumbled across it in a subfile of a subfile.

Here's a thing you may not know: it takes a long time to find a publisher. I'd written all of Night School before I even sent anything out to agents. Once I was signed by an agent, my agent and I edited the book for a couple of months before she took it out to publishers. It was then that we learned vampires and immortals were not going to be a thing people wanted. By that point, with the first book done and other people handling the publisher hunting, I'd had time to start working on book two. I had to throw away hundreds of pages of work from both books. It was *tough*, you guys. Months of work down the drain.

Now, though, I get to share it with you. So it was not all for nothing.

This excerpt is the opening from the unfinished second paranormal *Night School* novel. I don't have an outline for this book – I was winging it, back then. So, I'm not sure what I had planned for it. But I remember really liking how it started, and thinking that I really had something. It seemed to me that Allie discovering her witch powers was going to be *amazing*. And then the word came in that witch Allie was never going to see the light of day and work began on revising Night School into the book you know.

I think I used some of the feeling and the drama of this chapter in my only paranormal series, *The Secret Fire*. But most of it — all of it, really — has never been seen before by anyone. Not my agent. Not my publishers. Nobody. Until now.

It's a bit messy, the way all first drafts are. So forgive the occasional line that doesn't work, and the lack of detail. It's like a sketch for an oil painting — it's not complete. It's just a rough idea.

So have a look at what might have been. I was going to call book 2 Strange as Angels.

This is the last of the stories, by the way. It's been my pleasure to share these with you. As always, without you, there is no Night School Thank you for making it real. Thank you for being you.

Keep breathing.

CJx

"Do me a favour,

Rach. Don't tell

anybody anything

about this. Let's keep

this our secret."

December 1st

Keep moving and you won't die. Allie ran through the frozen woods, repeating those words in her head, over and over. *Keep moving.* Blue moonlight suffused the forest, glinting off her white pyjamas. *You won't die.*

Nobody was chasing her. Everybody knew to keep their distance now. But she ran anyway.

Nine hundred and seventy-one steps.

Nine hundred and seventy-two.

She clenched her hands into fists that pumped at her sides. She could hear nothing except her ragged breathing and the sound of her sodden slippers crunching through the snow.

In the full moon's glow, she could make out pine trees and frozen ferns as she skidded along the path. But all she could see was Rachel's face – the fear in her eyes.

Rachel had always been so fearless.

A sob welled up in Allie's throat and she forced it back.

Not now.

When the stone wall loomed out of the darkness. she nearly ran into it head-first. After forcing her frozen fingers to open the gate, she hurled herself across the churchyard to the chapel door. She shoved against it hard, but it gave easily and she fell onto the unforgiving stone floor of the sanctuary, crying out as pain shot through her shoulder.

After the bright moonlight, she could see nothing in the pitch-black chapel. Shivering violently, she felt the first waves of panic wash over her, but she knew she had to clear her mind. She needed not to feel anything.

Closing her eyes, she tried to think soothing thoughts. After a moment her breathing steadied, and she stumbled to her feet. She felt along the ancient walls for a light switch, but found only smooth, unyielding stone. She moved cautiously but still tripped in the darkness. White hot pain stabbed through her wounded shoulder, and she clutched her arm, tears in her eyes.

"Where are the LIGHTS?" she screamed at the ceiling, her voice echoing in the cold emptiness.

In an instant the room was suffused in the gentle glow cast by a thousand tiny white candles, floating in mid-air around her.

Allie turned in a slow circle, staring at them with blank incomprehension. Sobbing, she crumpled to the chapel floor. Immediately above her, she heard a strange hissing sound. She looked up to see a gentle rain fall from the ceiling. One by one, each candle went out, and disappeared.

The room plunged once again into darkness.

Soaked and trembling, Allie rocked on the floor, whispering hoarsely. "Make it stop. Make it stop. Make it stop. Make it stop..."

But the rain kept falling.

Three months earlier…

"Welcome to Cimmeria Academy. Could all new students please line up on the left? Returning students on the right."

Headmistress Isabelle le Fanult stood on a small, white platform at the end of the vast ballroom known as the Great Hall. She wasn't shouting, but her powerful voice soared clearly above the din of chattering students.

The room smelled of paint and varnish, but it was the first day of the autumn term, and the school looked fine. Better than fine. It had been polished to a high sheen. The freshly-painted white ceilings soared. The oak floors were so glossy Allie could see her reflection above as she and Rachel stood in the line on the right, studying the new students.

"They all look so young and nervous," Allie said. "Did I ever look like that?"

"Of course not, sweetie," Rachel said, flipping her long, curly ponytail over her shoulder. She called out to the new students. "Welcome to opening day, kittens. Isn't it awesome?"

Allie laughed nervously. She'd never been at Cimmeria during a full term. She'd started at the school in the summer when only a select group of students were enrolled. The autumn term brought back all the regular students as well as new ones, and she was already feeling overwhelmed.

"I knew there'd be more students in the autumn term, but I didn't know it would be like this," she admitted, raising her voice to be heard.

"Oh, Allie. You're still here. How wonderful for us."

Allie spun around to see a beautiful girl smiling sarcastically as the sunlight highlighted her long, red hair and illuminated her milky white skin.

169

"Oh bugger, it's Katy Gilmore." Allie covered her mouth dramatically. "Oops. I mean… Hi Katy. Welcome back."

Katy's perfect icy smile never wavered. "Imagine. You welcoming me back to the school I've been attending for three years. That's so *nouveau*." She walked out of the room without looking back.

Rachel made a sour face and pranced past Allie, swishing her hips in a representation of Katy's haughty stride. Flinging her hand out she drawled, "Oh Allie, why don't you just kill yourself for not being me?"

They were still giggling as they walked up to the registration table, but Allie's smile faded as she recognised August Zelazny sitting rifle straight, flipping through the pages of a clipboard. She had never got along with the history teacher. She'd hoped that after all they'd been through over the summer, he would warm to her. It hadn't happened.

"Sheridan. Patel," he barked. "Keep it down. Sheridan, you're in the same room you moved into over the summer term, 333. Patel, you're in the room next door, 335."

They exchanged excited glances, but he wasn't done. "If you act up or cause problems, you can lose this privilege and be moved to opposite sides of the dormitory. I don't want to see either of you in detention this term."

He handed each of them a thick envelope and looked past them. "Next!"

"He's so nice," Rachel whispered sweetly as they walked away.

"We're getting married," Allie said.

"How wonderful for you."

Giggling again, Rachel grabbed Allie's hand and pulled her over to the wall. Over the summer the 18th-century woodwork had been badly damaged by fire and a pitched battle. Workers had been in the room for weeks, and the repair was seamless. The elaborately-carved oak panelling looked precisely as it had before.

"How the hell did they…?" Rachel leaned over to peer more closely at the woodwork. "I'm sure it was right here."

Allie looked across the room at the headmistress, who caught her gaze and smiled knowingly.

"It's all … perfect," she said.

It felt like home.

As soon as she felt happy, though, her joy was washed away on a wave of guilt. She cast a sidelong glance at Rachel. She hadn't told her the truth yet about who she was. What she was. And she knew she had to. Rachel had been the one to tell her about the students and teachers here – that they were the children of immortals. That they would not all inherit their parents' genetic right to near-eternal life and superhuman powers. But some of them would.

Rachel had always played it straight with her, yet for several weeks Allie had been keeping the truth about herself a secret. For now, most of the students assumed she was one of them. She knew she wasn't.

This morning, she'd decided that the time had come to tell the truth to Rachel and Jo – her closest friends. She just wasn't sure how.

"Have you seen Carter today?" she asked, looking around.

Without losing a beat, Rachel pointed across the room towards the door, where Carter leaned against the wall, watching Allie steadily.

She turned to Rachel apologetically. "I have to talk to him. Catch you in a minute?"

Rachel nodded. "I'm going to move my stuff to my new room. After that, I have to be in the library right after lunch."

Allie feigned shock. "No. The library? I never would have guessed."

Rachel, who hoped to go to medical school, studied constantly.

"I know, right? I'm so boringly predictable"

"I'll come upstairs in a few and help you move." Allie headed across the room.

"Stalker!" Rachel called after.

Carter's dark eyes gave nothing away.

"Hey." She kicked lightly at his foot.

"Hey back," he said, ignoring the kick.

"Are you still coming up later?"

He nodded. "Oh yes. I'll be there."

"Cool. Don't forget."

"Oh, and good luck telling Rachel," he said, heading towards the registration table.

She stomped her foot. *"Will you please quit eavesdropping!"*

In her head, she heard him chuckle.

Since she and Carter discovered over the summer that they could communicate telepathically, they regularly conducted entire conversations without speaking aloud. Each had forbidden the other to eavesdrop, but they each cheated from time to time. Usually she could tell when he was listening to her thoughts, but if she wasn't paying attention he could sneak past her.

She hated it when he did that.

Still frowning, Allie walked slowly along the elegant, wood-panelled hallway and then up the grand central staircase with its smooth oak balustrade. Most of the students were still downstairs, and the sound of her footsteps echoed. She took her time, thinking about what she would say.

Rachel, it's like this. I might be a witch.

She climbed a second staircase, less grand than the first.

Rachel, I've been trying to decide how to tell you this. I know you don't believe in witches. OK, nobody does. Because they're not real. But, here's the thing…

She frowned to herself as she walked down a hallway to a small flight of stairs leading up to the dormitory floor.

"Rachel, I've been wanting to tell you something…"

Now down another narrow hallway painted white with a series of white doors leading off of it, each with a black number in the middle. She stopped in front of 378, her hand on the door handle.

See, this is going to sound really weird, but…

"Oh, for fucks sake. Would you quit practicing and just get on with it?"

Carter's voice in her head made her jump back from the door.

"Jesus. Don't do that!" she thought back sharply.

"Look. I know it's hard but it's driving you crazy keeping this secret." His voice was stern but not unsympathetic. *"So if you don't just go in there and tell her, I swear to God I'm going to tell her myself."*

At that moment, the door opened and Rachel rushed out – her arms filled with clothes piled as high as her head – slamming straight into Allie. They collapsed on the floor in a heap of dark blue school uniforms.

"Oh, hey Allie," Rachel said cheerfully as they scrambled to their feet. "Fancy running into you here."

"Sorry – I was just about to knock."

Rachel handed her an armload of shirts. "No worries. I was trying to defy physics. An accident was inevitable."

"*Good luck*." The chiding tone was gone from Carter's voice, and Allie felt a glow of warmth from him as she walked down to Rachel's new room.

Inside, clothes and bedding were piled in heaps. The single bed had not yet been made up, and Allie cleared a space and dropped her stack of clothing unceremoniously on the bare mattress.

"Hey," she said looking around, "isn't this room bigger than your last one?"

"I think so. And it has two bookcases, which I need. And a better view."

Allie walked to the desk to look out of the small arched window. Cimmeria sat at the foot of a steep hill, and emerald lawn rolled smoothly around it before being consumed by thick forest. The day was grey and cool, and faint wisps of fog swirled through the trees.

Allie started to speak, then changed her mind and began hanging dark blue skirts and crisp white blouses in the wardrobe, while Rachel filled the dresser drawers.

"I've still got, like, five boxes of books to move over," Rachel was saying as she worked. "But I only have one box. So, I'll have to fill and dump, fill and dump. It's going to be a lot of fun."

"That's great," Allie mumbled, completely missing Rachel's ironic tone.

She was so lost in thought that when Rachel said, "Earth to Allie, we have an emergency message for you," she only just noticed. When she looked up, Rachel was staring at her.

"Sorry," Allie said. "Up my own arse. What did I miss?"

Rachel studied her for a minute, then closed the dresser drawer and sat down in the desk chair.

"Right. Out with it."

Allie flushed. She wasn't ready.

"I don't know. I'm just..."

Rachel waved her hand dismissively. "Something's been bothering you all week. You're away with the fairies. Like, all the time. You look … I don't know. Wrong. So, out with it."

Allie sat down on the bed, holding a dark blue Cimmeria jumper tightly in her hands.

"Rach, I've been trying to figure out how to tell you something. Only, I don't think you're going to like it, so I haven't been able to do it."

"OK…" A frown creased Rachel's smooth forehead.

"You know how I went to my parents' house a couple of weeks ago?" Allie could hear the tension in her own voice. "Well, I went because Isabelle told me that I'm not… I'm not one of you. I'm not immortal." Allie looked down at her hands, which were twisting the sweater back and forth.

"I'm sorry, Allie." Rachel sounded genuinely sad.

Allie took a shaky breath and avoided looking at Rachel's face. "It's just… Well, there's more. Isabelle told me that I'm something else. Or at least, my grandmother was something else. I might be, too."

Rachel sat very still, her eyes searching Allie's face for clues.

Allie took a deep breath, then the words tumbled out so quickly that they all rushed together. "Isabelle says that my grandmother and my great-grandmother   were   witches. PossiblytheonlyonesintheworldandIcouldbeone … too."

The room was quiet for a long moment, as Rachel seemed to struggle for something to say.

"But Allie," she said finally, her voice studiedly calm, "that's impossible. There's no such thing as witches. You know that."

"I know," Allie said, her cheeks reddening. "But Isabelle says… she says there is. Or at least, there were. But I might not have inherited my grandmother's powers. And there's no way to know unless I start turning boys into toads or something because we need my grandmother's book – her journal, basically – to know how this whole thing works. And I can't find it anywhere."

For a few seconds. Rachel sat where she was. Then she stood up and started folding clothes again as if nothing had happened.

"Isabelle has been wrong about things, you know," she said matter-of-factly. "She's not perfect. And I absolutely do not believe in witches. But if it turns out that you are, then fine. You are. And if you're not, which is more likely, then you're human. And that's also fine. Either way, you're Allie." She closed a drawer emphatically.

Allie dropped the sweater and ran over to hug her tightly. She'd known rational, pragmatic Rachel would find this all hard to believe. And she could tell that she wasn't convinced.

But at least she wasn't freaking out.

"Hey, if it turns out that you are a witch I want you to cast a spell to help me pass advanced biology," Rachel said, opening another drawer. "Because I've looked at that textbook and it is a be-atch."

Laughing, Allie threw a sock at her. Then she thought of something, and she stopped laughing. "Do me a favour, Rach. Don't tell anybody anything about this. Let's keep it our secret. If people like Katy and her group find out, they'll harass me constantly."

Rachel folded a T-shirt into a tiny square. Her face was suddenly serious, as if she were thinking about something else. Something dangerous.

"Rachel?" Allie nudged her. "Keep it a secret?"

Rachel met her gaze – Allie had never seen her look more anxious.

"Forever," she said. "No one can ever know."

***

Allie helped Rachel move, arrange and then rearrange her new room for the next hour, and they never mentioned the subject again. She wasn't certain this was a good sign, and she was still fretting about it as she hurried down to the dining room for lunch.

Meal times at Cimmeria were strict – if you arrived too late, you didn't eat. And yet, even though she was cutting it close, Allie still stopped just inside the dining room door to take in the scene. Towering windows on the far wall let in grey daylight, softly illuminating the spacious room where the ceilings were nearly as high as those in the Great Hall. During the summer term, it had held just ten round tables, each surrounded by eight carved, wooden chairs. At that time, much of the room was barely used. Even now, with twice as many tables, there was space to spare. But it felt crowded to Allie, and the noise made by more than a hundred students was daunting.

A slim, girl with short, sleek blonde hair waved at her enthusiastically from a table near the massive, stone fireplace.

"Allie! Over here!"

Allie made her way across the room to the table where Jo sat ignoring everyone around her, none of whom Allie recognised. She patted the empty seat next to her. "I saved you a place so you wouldn't starve. It's bonkers in here."

Allie swung her arm to take in the room and pretended she had to shout above the din. "Where did they all come from?"

Jo laughed. "I know! How different is this from summer term? The place is packed. The cheeky buggers even took our table."

She pointed at the spot in the middle of the room where they usually sat with a group of friends. It was now occupied by fresh-faced 14-year-olds, talking to each other awkwardly.

"I didn't have the heart to move them," Jo said. "They're just babies. I'll break the news to them later. Gently."

She dipped her spoon into a white bowl filled with blood-red soup. "As long as they're out of there by tomorrow they can live. How's it going, anyway?"

"What is that? Tomato?" Allie asked, studying Jo's soup.

"Yes, but I think it has beet in it. It's the colour of carnage."

Cimmeria's kitchen staff were quite good cooks, but sometimes their experiments didn't work out.

Allie took half a sandwich off a tray in the middle of the table and ladled some soup from a large, porcelain tureen into one of the bowls stacked neatly beside it.

"Sorry I'm late. I got distracted."

"As usual." Jo smiled.

"Did you keep your same room?" Allie asked. "I'm in Katy's room. Well, I guess it's my room now."

"Oh God, check under the floorboards," Jo said with a grimace. "She'll have left plutonium somewhere. Yep, I'm staying where I was last term, thank God. Couldn't face moving. I'm far too lazy."

Allie looked around the crowded room. "Just a physics question here. There were only so many empty rooms in the girls' wing over the summer. Where's everyone going to sleep?"

Jo pointed downwards. "There's a mezzanine floor below our dorm. The younger girls will be there. They don't open it in the summer."

"This place goes on forever," Allie muttered, sipping her soup and squinting as she tried to decide if she liked it.

"It shrinks in the summer and expands in the autumn. Fact." Jo pushed her soup bowl away, wrinkling her nose. "That was weird. Hey, what's your course timetable like? Are you in my classes?" She held out her hand. "Give it."

Allie shoved the last quarter of sandwich into her mouth, then dug around her bag until she found the white slip of paper. "Here," she mumbled through her food.

"You're such a lady." Jo unfolded it. As she read, she brightened. "We're in three classes together this term! History, Biology and French. This is brilliant." She blinked at Allie over the top of the paper. "I wonder if I could convince Isabelle to move us together for everything. I could promise to be good. For the first time ever."

"You'd get sick of me," Allie said. "I snore."

"That is so not a surprise." Jo handed her schedule back.

"Hang on." Allie looked up from her soup. "How can we have French together? I thought you were in advanced French?"

Jo smiled, picking up her bag. "I think you'll find that you, too, are in advanced French, *ma petite chou*."

Allie stared at her. "No way."

"And in advanced History, Biology and English."

"No. Way."

Jo rolled her eyes. "Allie-cat, haven't you looked at your own timetable?"

Quickly, Allie scanned the paper. Jo was right. For two years her grades had been sliding, but all her recent hard work had paid off.

"Unfortunately, you're still in normal baby Maths," Jo said, smugly bursting her bubble. "Which is lame." She stood, grabbing her bag. "Are you coming?"

Allie laughed. "Maybe. Depends on where you're going."

Jo was already walking away so her reply floated back over her shoulder. "Common room. To pee around my favourite sofa so the little ones don't try to steal that too."

Taking the rest of her sandwich with her, Allie followed her out. After the clamour of the dining room, the hallway was a peaceful oasis. She couldn't help but notice the sheer vigour with which the school building had been prepared for opening day – the wood floors gleamed, the oil paintings shone.

The common room, reached through a door just beside the main staircase, was lined with bookcases and filled with deep leather sofas, chairs and ottomans. A grand piano dominated one corner. There was no television – Cimmeria allowed no modern electronics.

Jo plopped onto her favourite sofa with a satisfied sigh. "None of those damned ankle biters are getting my spot." She stretched languorously. "I can't believe classes start tomorrow. Summer term – and all of that bollocks – seriously just ended. Like, a week ago."

Allie sat at the other end of the sofa, her legs curled up beneath her. "Totally. None of that counted as a break."

Jo picked up a fashion magazine from a nearby table and flipped through the pages, glancing half-heartedly at the pictures. "Have you met any of the new students yet?" she asked, admiring a pricy designer dress.

Jo's parents were very wealthy and, when it came to material goods, she wanted for nothing. But money was pretty much all her parents showered her with.

Allie shook her head. "Not yet. They've only just arrived, and I've been busy. Are there any I should know about?"

"Well, the younger ones, I don't know. But…" She closed the magazine and put it back on the table. "Of the returning students, there are a few worth mentioning. I saw Caro in the hallway today. Caro Thompkins. She was here for a while this summer, but she left when … everything happened."

Allie tried to remember her but came up empty. It must have shown on her face because Jo kept describing her.

"She's a friend of Carter's," she said, a bit cautiously. "You remember – he took her to the summer ball."

A moment played out in Allie's mind. Carter standing in the grand ballroom as an orchestra began to play, looking elegant in black-tie, his face concerned, his eyes dark as the night outside. He was warning her not to trust her date, Sylvain le Qualien. He'd had his arm around a girl who gazed up at him adoringly.

"Pretty? Blonde? Small?"

Jo nodded. She looked like she was trying to think of the right thing to say. "She's actually kind of cool. I think you'd like her."

Allie was surprised by the hot rush of jealousy that swept through her.

It had been her own decision that she and Carter should be friends and nothing more. She knew he he'd wanted more, but she'd pushed him away. Not because she didn't like him back, but because she didn't know how she felt about anything anymore. About him. About Sylvain.

Jo was watching alertly, waiting for a response.

"That's cool," she said finally, trying to hide her confused emotions. "I'll look out for her, I guess." She glanced at her watch and feigned concern. "I'd better dash."

It was only two o'clock; she wasn't meeting Carter for an hour still, but suddenly she needed some time to think before she saw him.

With a shrug, Jo picked up the magazine again. "See you at dinner?"

"Totally."

She hurried out of the common room, passing a gaggle of young students who stood in the doorway looking around wonderingly.

"No TVs," one of them was saying. "I might die."

"No computers," another replied in tones of quiet desperation. "Seriously. What the hell will we do?"

***

Up three flights of stairs, her mind whirled. What was Jo trying to tell her? Was she saying that Carter had a girlfriend?

That wasn't possible.

Suddenly she winced. She'd forgotten for a moment that Carter had been eavesdropping a lot lately. But over the summer he'd taught her how to protect her thoughts from intrusion – by him or anybody else. They called it 'shutting the door'.

She did it now with the merest flick of a thought.

She'd reached her room, and hurried into the quiet, small space. With its white-washed walls and white bed linen, she always thought it looked like heaven. Or a hospital. Here, behind the solid barricade she created around her thoughts, she could fret in peace.

She sat down on the bed, then almost immediately got back on her feet and began pacing the room.

From the moment she'd met Carter, they'd felt a connection to each other. He was, she had to admit, amazing-looking – tall, with a dark shock of thick hair and deep, brown eyes. He had a killer smile although he almost never deployed it – it made his eyes crinkle at the edges adorably. And he had a rich, baritone voice that rumbled through her.

And yet.

He was her best guy friend. They had been, for most of the summer, inseparable. They could just hang out in easy silence for hours. If they got together she'd lose that easiness, she was certain of it. And if they ever broke up – and of course they would -- she'd lose him altogether.

And that would be the end of Carter and Allie.

She sighed and spun on her heel, pacing the other way.

Nine steps across, nine steps back.

On the other hand, of course, there was Sylvain, with his café au lait skin and blue, blue eyes. He'd used his powers to force her to fancy him.

After that she'd loathed him. But he had worked hard to prove he was really sorry. And he'd saved her life more than once. Without him, she wouldn't be here right now.

But she could never trust him. Not completely. Not after last summer. *And yet.*

There was something about him. All he had to do was touch her and she melted. Even thinking about him now made her flush.

"Oh grow up, Allie," she hissed at herself.

She opened the window to let in fresh air and stopped, staring at the object on her desk. For the thousandth time she pressed her fingers along the top, but it wouldn't open. It just didn't make sense...

Someone knocked on the door and she jumped. As she turned around, it swung open. Carter leaned against the door frame, studying her. His demeanour was relaxed but she could sense his alertness.

"You rang?"

"You're early."

They each spoke at the same time.

He raised an eyebrow and glanced at his watch. "How rude of me. Should I wait in the corridor until three precisely?"

"Don't be an idiot." She said it more impatiently than she'd meant. "Come in. Close the door."

He did as she said, then leaned against the wall, his arms crossed loosely but protectively across his chest.

"What's up?"

Allie got up and went to stand closer to him. "It's just..." She took a step back and pointed at her desk. "Look. Here it is."

A wooden box sat on top of it. The size of a jewellery box, it was made of a rich, golden-red wood, covered in an elaborate constellation of carved stars.

"Blimey." Carter walked over and reached for it. "Can I..."

Allie nodded her assent, and he lifted it to examine it.

"It's beautiful," he said. "Hand-made. Cedar. Somebody must have worked on this for ages.. I've never seen anything like it."

"I can't even find a lock," Allie said. "Much less open it."

He twisted and turned it, searching for a latch that wasn't there. He stared at it, fascinated. "I can't see hinges."

"Exactly."

He set it down and sat in the desk chair. After a moment's hesitation, Allie sat down on the bed across from him.

"Tell me again what happened at home." He leaned forward so that his forearms rested on his muscular thighs. "Everything you saw. What was around it when you found it. Where it was. How your parents reacted. Everything."

Allie was surprised by his forensic enthusiasm, but she knew he must have a reason. He always did.

"OK," she said. "Well, as I'd expected, my mum was completely freaked out that I knew about my grandmother being a witch. She's in total denial."

She pulled her feet up onto the bed and rested her chin on her knees, remembering.

Three weeks earlier…

It started out OK. Her parents were both so happy to see her. Even after everything that had happened – and all that Allie had learned over the summer at Cimmeria – the awkwardness since Christopher had run away was now not so obvious.

In fact, the car journey from Cimmeria to London had been filled with lively conversation. They'd peppered her with questions about school, her classes, her teachers. Given that she'd just found herself in the middle of a battle – actual hand-to-hand combat with immortals – it felt strange to talk about how she'd got an A in Biology. But it also felt wonderfully normal. And for a brief, fleeting moment, normal felt good.

So, she told them about her grades, and about Rachel, Jo and Carter (but not Sylvain). And then suddenly they were driving up their ordinary south London street, and the two-hour journey was over.

The house looked wonderfully unchanged. Her room had been cleaned, but otherwise was just as she'd left it the day she first went to Cimmeria. She'd plopped down on the bed, looking around at the posters – it seemed like years ago that she'd put them up. Her MP3 player lay on top of the desk and she caressed it lightly before opening the top drawer to find her laptop nestled in its usual place.

She thought for a second she might cry and she had to laugh at her own reaction.

Never thought I'd be so emotional about a piece of metal.

They'd avoided sensitive topics all through dinner and afterwards she'd just sat in front of the TV, flipping channels – absorbing the frenetic sound and hyper-real colours. But after months without it, the banality and canned laughter she'd always found so comforting seemed jarring. In the end, she'd switched it off.

She saw her parents exchange one of those "Did you see that?" looks.

"There's nothing on, really," she'd told them, squirming in the warmth of their approving gaze. The pleasantness had lasted until the next morning.

After tea, toast, and cosy chitchat in the family kitchen, Allie decided it was time to talk. Her father had gone to the shop for more milk. Her mother was washing the breakfast dishes, humming to herself.

"Mum, I need to know about my grandmother." Her tone was tentative but firm – and looking back she still couldn't see a better way in which she could have broached the subject. Nonetheless, she felt as if she'd accidentally switched off a light on a dark day.

Her mother froze, a soapy mug in one hand. The sound of running water seemed loud. Allie watched with worried eyes – she'd expected something, but not this sudden... nothing.

After a long few seconds, her mother turned off the water, set the cup down and stripped off her yellow rubber gloves. Turning her back to the sink, she said, "There's not much to tell you, Allie. I didn't know her very well."

"But you knew she was a witch."

The last word made her mother wince. "Yes," she said, dryly. "I did know that."

"And she sent you to Cimmeria."

"Yes."

Allie waited for her mother to volunteer more, but she stood stubbornly mute.

She tried again. "And then after that you moved to London and left her ... all of that behind?"

"It wasn't the life I wanted."

Allie was surprised to hear a touch of adolescent defiance in her mother's voice.

"Did you ever see my grandmother again?"

Her mother began putting the dishes away, cris-crossing the kitchen with quick steps, her face turned away from Allie. "Not for a long time." Her voice held a new note. Something like regret. "I didn't see her for about five years after I left school. Then one day she showed up without warning, as if nothing had happened. After that, she would pop in from time to time, usually when I was busy." She paused, holding a plate. "She showed up all the time when I was pregnant with you. I thought back then... Well. It seemed to me she was obsessed with you."

Allie, who had never heard any of this before, stared. "Obsessed with me? How do you mean?"

"She knew you were a girl from the very start. She used to talk to you in the womb – it drove me crazy. She was always whispering 'Hello, little girl...' to my belly. I guess it was the only time we were ever close. Pregnancy was the only thing we'd ever had in common." She set the plate down gently, a slight smile on her face. "After you were born, she was around quite a bit. She'd show up and help out for a week or so – she loved feeding you and pushing you in your pram – and then she'd disappear again. Then, when you were about three, she went away and never came back. I heard nothing at all from her. It was more than a year later that I heard about her death."

Allie looked out of the window, into the grey light, imagining her mother young and pretty, and her mysterious grandmother, pushing a baby in a stroller, feeding her with a bottle... It seemed so strange that she would just walk away from that and then...

"How did she die?"

Her mother shook her head. "I still have no idea. I received a call from a man who identified himself as 'an associate' of hers. He said that she'd... died and he needed my address so he could send me the death certificate. He refused to say anything else. The certificate arrived a week later. It had been issued in Scotland. But that's all the information I had. To this day I don't know where she's buried."

Allie tried to imagine not knowing how or where your own mother had died. The very thought made her heart ache.

"Did she leave anything behind? Any of her things?"

Her mother hesitated, for a long time before replying. "About two weeks after I received that phone call, a van pulled up outside the house. The driver had instructions to bring her things here. He was just a delivery man – he didn't know who had sent him." She looked away. "He had quite a few boxes. We put them all up in the loft. I've never looked at them again."

Allie couldn't believe her luck – what she was looking for might have been in her house all along. She leaned forwards urgently. "I need to see her things."

Her mother crossed her arms across her chest. The warmth between them cooled. "I don't like the idea of you getting all tangled up in that world, Allie. Not after what it did to your grandmother." Her face was calm but Allie could see sadness in her eyes. "It destroyed her family. And her life." She added, almost as an afterthought, "And mine."

For a second, her mother looked so vulnerable that it tugged at Allie's heart, but sympathy was followed by a quick fire of outrage.

"Hang on – *you* sent me to Cimmeria, the school you hated so much. You knew I would meet these people. That I would learn who I was."

Her mother moved to speak but Allie held up her hand.

"You must have known this would happen. So don't tell me now that you don't want me to get mixed up in that world," she finished icily. "You threw me into that world."

Her mother rubbed her temples, and for the first time Allie noticed the circles under her eyes. She looked tired. "I didn't have any choice, Allie," she said. "It was the least worst option for you. After Christopher left, you went out of control. I had to do something. I couldn't lose both my children…"

Her voice trailed off, and she took a deep breath. "I knew, if nothing else, Isabelle would keep you safe. I also knew that you'd learn the truth. I decided it was worth it." She held her hands out. "So, here we are."

The anger left Allie as suddenly as it had arrived. "Mum, look. I don't know if I'm like my grandmother. But if I am, I'm going to need your help. And I'm going to need her help."

Her mother's hands jerked reflexively, and she wound her fingers together tightly.

Allie continued. "I promise you I'm not Christopher, and you're not going to lose me. But I need to see Grandmother's things. I have to see them."

After a second, her mother's shoulders drooped.

"Well, you may as well," she said, her voice so low Allie could barely hear her. "After all, she sent it all to you."

Allie stared. "What do you mean, she sent it to me?"

Her mother walked back to the sink and stood with her back to Allie.

"The packing slip, when the boxes were delivered. It wasn't in my name." She pulled her rubber gloves on with angry snaps. "It was in yours."

"Oh now, that's very interesting," Carter said, as she reached that point in the story. "How old were you at the time?"

"Four."

They held each other's eyes, both thinking the same thing. Allie broke the silence.

"So that afternoon Dad and I went up into the attic."

"Was he cross about it, like your mum?"

"No. He seemed almost eager to show me. Even, like, excited. And something else – he seemed really familiar with all of the boxes. I got the feeling this wasn't the first time he'd looked at them."

She told him how that afternoon, her dad had opened the loft hatch and pulled down the foldout ladder. He'd climbed up first and flipped on the light and she'd clambered up after him. The attic floor had been made up of bare floorboards, the peaked roof just high enough for them to stand up straight. A cloud of dust motes had floated in the harsh light of the bare bulb.

Allie had sneezed.

"Dusty," her father had observed mildly, already moving towards the left side of the attic. "Now let's see. I think they're right over… Yes. Here they are."

"He found the boxes immediately," Allie told Carter. "And the loft is kind of crowded with junk – our old toys, paddling pools, boxes of rubbish. I don't think he could have found the Christmas decorations that quickly and we use those every year."

Carter nodded. "So how many boxes were there?"

"Eight."

"Were they sealed?"

She tilted her head to one side as she thought about it. "Yes and no. They were taped shut, but the tape gave way easily. And some boxes seemed to have fresh tape – different than the others. But there was something else."

He raised an eyebrow.

"Everything in the attic was super dusty. But those boxes had no dust on them at all."

Allie's father had pulled open the first box and set it down for her.

It had been filled with clothes. She'd pulled out a vividly-coloured piece of chiffon that had turned out to be a 1970s-style dress, long and flowing, with a jewelled collar.

"Whoa! Grandmother was on trend," she'd said.

"Oh, yes. Your grandmother loved a party…"

"Frankly, the whole thing was just weird," she told Carter. "Dad was practically bouncing on his toes in the attic. He'd seemed excited."

"What happened next?" Carter said. "You found clothes in that box. Then?"

"It was more than just clothes," Allie replied. She'd found one expensive gown after another – some floaty chiffon, others heavily beaded

– all with designer names that Allie vaguely recognised from celebrity magazines.

In amongst the dresses were ropes of pearls, sparkling earrings that could have been diamonds, rings with big, chunky stones.

She'd held up a black pearl bracelet and looked at her father. "Dad, this stuff looks really valuable. Was Grandmother minted, or what?"

His laugh had been almost giddy. "Oh yes. And she was generous. We'd never have been able to buy this house without her help." He'd handed Allie another box.

That one had been filled with more clothes. Amongst the frocks and jewellery, little crystal jars had been wrapped protectively in scarves. Allie had pulled the stopper from one and sniffed it curiously – it had smelled like a garden after the rain. Cool and fresh. For a second she'd thought she felt a raindrop on her face. Startled, she'd looked up at the attic roof, but there was no sign of a leak.

She'd set the jars to one side, along with a cobalt silk scarf that had caught her eye.

Everything else, she'd carefully repacked.

One after another, she'd gone through the boxes finding much the same things. Expensive clothes, a crimson velvet throw, painted porcelain jars, more jewellery, and long, silk evening gloves.

The last box had been heavy – her father had carried it carefully and set it down with a clunk. Allie had parted the cardboard to find stacks of antique books with old leather bindings in rich colours of earth and cognac.

"Some were in French, others in Latin. One was in Greek – or at least my dad said it was Greek. I didn't know what it was," she told Carter. "Only a couple were in English, and they were history books – *The Rise and Fall of the Roman Empire*, that sort of thing."

"Where did you find the casket?" he asked, touching it lightly.

"At the bottom of that box of books."

It was the last thing they'd found. She'd pulled it out and run her fingers across the heavily carved lid.

"What do you suppose this is?" she'd asked her father.

He'd taken it from her and turned it around. His hands had trembled. He looked strange, she'd thought. The presence of the box seemed to baffle him. Even, perhaps, scare him.

"I have no idea," he'd said slowly. "I've never seen it before."

He'd pulled at the top ineffectually, and turned it over in his hands, looking for a catch. "I can't see how this opens."

"Let me try." She'd held out her hands, but he'd hesitated a long moment before handing it to her.

Allie hadn't been able to open it either, and eventually they'd packed everything back up. Her father had carried a single box downstairs for her.

Along with the box of books, Allie had kept the crystal bottles, the velvet throw, the box that wouldn't open, and a single dress of gossamer silk.

"Those are the bottles." She pointed at a row of small crystal bottles glittering on one of the narrow shelves of the white bookcase near her bed.

Carter pulled the stopper out of one and sniffed it carefully.

He looked up at her, surprised. "That's so strange – it's not like perfume. Check it out. It's incredible."

He held the bottle out and Allie sniffed it, her hand resting lightly on his wrist. A scent of night filled her nose – cool air, damp soil, moon overhead. She could feel a fresh breeze toy with her hair.

"I know," she said, looking up at him. "I don't think they are perfumes. I think they're something else. I just don't know what."

She noticed goosebumps on his skin, and was suddenly conscious of how close they were to each other. She jerked her hand away.

Instantly, his mood darkened and he smiled sardonically. His expression was dangerous. "Oh, I'm sorry. Did I burn you?"

Flustered, she took a step back. "No, don't be… I just…"

"Never mind, Allie," he sighed, stoppering the crystal jar and setting it gently back on the shelf. "It doesn't matter."

A heavy silence divided them, and Allie rushed to fill it.

"So," she said, leaning with elaborate casualness against the wall near the door, "to sum up: no journal. Nothing even sort of like a journal."

Carter stared out of the window, his back to her. "And you said your parents were behaving strangely?"

"Honestly? I think they'd both been through those boxes before – maybe more than once. My dad knew that stuff well. He was acting so guilty."

"So they're lying to you." Carter's voice was emotionless.

"Again."

"And we're right where we started."

Allie shook her head. "I don't know about that. I don't think anything was in those boxes by chance. My grandmother sent them to me for a reason." She hesitated. "And something tells me that wooden casket is important."

***

At 6:55 p.m., Allie, Jo and Rachel joined the raucous crowd hurrying down the main staircase.

"Who are these people?" Jo asked grumpily as someone jostled past her.

"Calm down, newbies!" Rachel called out in her most parental tone, but it had no effect on the boisterous throng.

When they reached the dining hall, though, the new students hushed in awe. The room had undergone its magical nightly transformation – the chandeliers were dimmed, the tables bedecked with white linens and sparkling candles. Each place setting held glittering crystal glasses and white china plates with the dark blue Cimmeria crest in the centre.

Jo wound her way smoothly through the spellbound students. Rachel and Allie followed in her wake. Gabe and Lucas were fiercely guarding their usual table, and Gabe spread his arms wide as they approached, his white teeth gleaming as he smiled.

"Your table, mademoiselles," he said.

"Brilliant," Jo said, pulling out the chair next to his. "We'll just take turns getting here early until the young ones learn the rules."

Gabe leaned over to whisper something to her, and she smiled up at him. Allie was relieved to see them so comfortable together – they'd been a couple until a month ago. Their breakup had been particularly brutal. At least, they were friends again.

Across the table Lucas watched them guardedly, his dark hair falling forwards so it nearly covered his eyes. His ill-considered summer fling with Jo might be over, but they were all still dealing with the fallout.

At that thought, Allie turned to scan the room. "Has anyone seen Lisa?"

"Nobody 'sees' Lisa anymore," Gabe said dramatically. "They just feel it when she breaks their necks."

"There she is." Rachel pointed towards the door where a small, athletic girl with very short dark hair was looking around alertly. Allie and Jo waved to get her attention, and she strode over to them, slipping into a chair without a word.

She didn't look at Lucas.

Conversation dried up, all of them aware of what had happened to Lisa. She'd been attacked and bitten by an immortal. The venom from that bite had changed her utterly from a fragile, sweet girl into a ruthless and powerful fighter.

Rachel turned to Lucas to ask him a seemingly spontaneous question about their biology teacher, smoothly defusing the tension.

"Is this seat taken?" Carter's voice startled Allie, and she nearly elbowed him as he pulled out the chair next to her.

"Sorry," she said, feeling bewildered. "I mean..." He simply never sat with them. Ever. "No?" she said slowly.

"These new kids are screwing everything up," he muttered as he sat down. "I hate the autumn term."

"Did the little bastards get your table?" Gabe asked. "They took ours at lunch. Somebody's going to have to explain how this all works."

"They'll learn."

Lisa's voice was so unexpected that it momentarily quieted the discussion again.

"Yes, of course they will," Jo chirped.

Allie turned to smile at her but stopped abruptly. Sylvain had slipped stealthily into the last empty chair at the table. As she gaped, the others turned to see what she was looking at. Silence fell.

Noticing their attention, Sylvain shrugged nonchalantly and gestured at the rest of the room. "This place, it is not normal tonight." His French accent made the comment inherently charming, and he smiled dazzlingly at them all. Nobody seemed to know quite how to respond.

"Well," Rachel said with determined enthusiasm, "I guess, after last summer, you could call this the survivors' table."

Allie could see Carter and Lisa watching Rachel quizzically. Then Gabe spoke up.

"Rachel's right. We don't always get along. But none of us would be here now if it weren't for the others."

"Exactly." Rachel looked pleased. "I think this moment deserves a toast.

She held up her water glass. After a second, Allie, Gabe and Jo picked up their glasses, and the others gradually followed, although Carter and Lisa joined in with obvious reluctance.

"To the survivors of the summer term!" Rachel said.

"The survivors," they chorused.

"Oh good," Jo said, sounding relieved. "Dinner at last."

The doors at the end of the dining hall had opened and black-clad waiters streamed in carrying steaming platters of food on enormous trays.

As the food was passed around, conversation at the table fractured naturally into small groupings.

Allie turned to Carter. "Have you got Jerry for Biology again? And Mrs Watson for English?"

He nodded. "I can't wait," he said ironically.

Conscious of Sylvain's presence, she glanced up to find him staring at her.

"What?" she mouthed at him.

He didn't respond, and after a moment he looked away.

From across the table, Rachel raised an eyebrow at her. Allie rolled her eyes in Sylvain's direction and Rachel gave her a knowing look before returning her focus to what Lucas was telling her.

Allie stabbed her fork into a piece of chicken.

"Sylvain still fancies you."

Hearing his voice in her head, Allie turned to look at Carter, but his attention appeared to be on his plate as he ate steadily.

"Yeah, well. There's not much I can do about that." She ate without much pleasure.

"Do you fancy him?"

She choked on her food and, coughing, grabbed her water glass. Jo pounded on her back helpfully.

"You OK?" she asked.

Allie nodded, admonishing herself again for not telling Jo about the witch thing, then turned back to Carter. Her eyes narrowed.

"I can't believe you're asking me that question."

"I notice that you're not answering." His tone was clipped.

"I'm not answering because ... because…" She sputtered as she tried to decide why she wasn't answering. *"It's none of your business."*

He glanced up and his eyes flickered across hers.

"Uh-huh."

"You're quiet tonight, Allie," Jo said. "Is everything OK?"

Reluctantly, Allie turned her attention away from Carter, who was still, to anyone else watching, eating with pleasure.

"Sorry," she said, with a distracted half-smile. "I'm lost in thought."

***

"I can't believe he asked you that. What did you say back? Ancient Greek, over to the left."

Jo reached up to hand Allie a slim book with a tattered leather cover. The numbered sticker on the binding was just barely hanging on, and as she climbed up the rolling ladder Allie rubbed her thumb over it to stick it down. They were at the very back of the library, in a section used primarily by teachers and advanced students. When she reached the top of the ladder, Allie was more than fifteen feet up – above the light fixtures and slightly obscured in the shadows.

They'd been volunteering in the library ever since last summer's battle had left the room damaged, with thousands of books thrown out of place. Now, though, it was all nearly back to normal.

"I told him it was none of his business." Her voice floated down to Jo, disembodied.

"Good for you," Jo called up. "What did he say to that?"

Allie stretched to put the book in its place on the shelf, then climbed down the polished wooden ladder and sat on one of the lower rungs.

"Nothing," she said. "He just gave me one of those looks."

Jo made a face. "How annoying."

"So annoying."

"More Greek." Jo handed her two more books.

As Allie climbed back up again, Jo watched her go. When she was just out of view Jo called after her. "Here's the thing, though. Do you fancy Sylvain?" She ducked behind a shelf, peering up at Allie from beneath it.

"Oh, for God's sake," Allie complained. "Not you, too?" She shoved the book into place with more violence than was strictly necessary.

"Don't freak out," Jo said quickly. "I'm totally on your side. I just don't know which side that is."

Allie climbed back down. She picked up one of the last books from a wooden cart and flipped its pages without looking at them.

"The problem is, I like them both. In different ways. And I don't want to choose. I know it sounds weird, but..." She shrugged helplessly. "I want them both."

"Blimey." Jo leaned back against the Anglo-Saxon shelf. "That'll never work."

"I know." Allie closed the book with a snap.

Jo studied her soberly. "What are you going to do?"

"Not a clue," Allie replied, shoving the book into an empty spot.

It popped out again instantly and she had to jump to catch it.

"What the...?" She shoved it back into the same spot, but this time it simply wouldn't go in.

She reached her hand into the space on the shelf and felt behind it – there was nothing blocking it. Lifting the book up, she examined it curiously.

"This one hasn't got a label. It must have fallen off."

"What is it?" Jo asked.

Allie studied the cover. "No idea. Something latiny, greeky..."

Laughing, Jo took it from her and glanced at the title before handing it back.

"What do they teach kids these days? It's an old book of Latin phrases. Hang onto it. We'll ask Eloise to make it a new sticker."

They shelved the last books from the cart then headed back to the front of the room. Tucking the book under her arm, Allie walked over to talk to Rachel, who sat studying in a pool of golden light at one of the large wooden tables scattered around the room. The light made her dark hair glisten, and her almond-shaped eyes gleamed.

"How's the Chemistry or Biology or whatever?" Allie asked.

"Fascinating," Rachel replied with real enthusiasm.

"Freak."

"That's not my name." She stood up and stretched. "I was about to head up. It's nearly curfew. You done?"

Allie nodded, and Rachel gestured at the stacks of books beside her. "Would you mind helping me? I'm defying physics again."

"No problem." Allie scooped up an armload of books. "Let's get out of here. I'm already sick of libraries, and classes don't start until tomorrow."

"I love libraries," Rachel said as they walked out the door.

"You know, Rachel, nobody likes a show-off."

Upstairs, Allie dropped Rachel's books onto her desk and headed for the door.

"Hang on," Rachel called after her. "This one's not mine."

Allie took the book of Latin phrases from her hand.

"Bugger. I meant to give this to Eloise." She shrugged and hurried out the door. "Guess I'll give it to her tomorrow. Last one to the bathroom's Zelazny's girlfriend."

Later, after she'd washed her face and put on her pyjamas, she picked the small, leather-bound book up off her desk and flipped through it again. She'd never studied Latin, so its words were meaningless to her, and after a moment she tossed it down carelessly next to the wooden casket on her desk and began organising her notebooks and papers for the next day.

A cool breeze blew through the room, ruffling the papers in her hands. On the desk to her left, the book flipped open, its pages rustling and turning.

Instinctively, Allie reached up to shut the window. But it was already shut. And securely latched.

She spun around to look at the door across the room, but it was closed tight as well.

Slowly, she turned her gaze back to the book, which now lay open on her desk. The paper was ivory with age, but the ink was as dark as if it had been written the day before. Cautiously, she ran her finger down the page reading the incomprehensible phrases; sounding them out. Her voice was hesitant but curious. None of it made any sense. Just vowels and consonants. The ancient words might as well have been pretend for all it meant to her. But she enjoyed reading them. Something about them was strangely pleasing. There was a comforting ring of the words. Almost familiar. And she had the strangest feeling the book *wanted* her to read them. It wanted her to continue.

She turned a page and began a new sentence, still not sure why she was doing it.

"*Iacta alea est...*" she said.

Abruptly, the book slammed shut, narrowly missing her fingers.

Jumping back as if she'd been burned, Allie stared at the book, still on her desk. Nothing but leather and paper. The breeze was gone from the air. Everything was perfectly innocent.

"What the hell," she murmured, "is going on?"

Links

Follow C. J. DAUGHERTY on…

INSTAGRAM @cj_daugherty
YOUTUBE /nightschoolbook
TWITTER @cj_daugherty

Join her book club at…

www.christidaugherty.com

Christi●Daugherty

Printed in Great Britain
by Amazon